C000137843

Quantum Chronicles
In the
Eleventh Dimension
2

Within the Eleventh Dimension
Both Time & Chronology Cease To Be
And A Myriad Of Impossibilities Become Possible....

"*All the stories are excellent and provide much food for thought but the two (The Appointment/Memoirs of Time) are, for me at least, outstanding in both content and the implications they contain for us all now in this very real materialistic world of ours...*"

Professor Jeremy Dunning Davies

13 short stories

Quantum
Chronicles
In The Eleventh
Dimension
2

Anthony Fucilla

Published 2011 by arima publishing

www.arimapublishing.com

ISBN 978 1 84549 507 7

© Anthony Fucilla 2011

All rights reserved

This book is copyright. Subject to statutory exception and to provisions of relevant collective licensing agreements, no part of this publication may be reproduced, stored in a retrieval system, or transmitted in any form or by any means, without the prior written permission of the author.

Printed and bound in the United Kingdom

Typeset in Garamond 11/14

This book is sold subject to the conditions that it shall not, by way of trade or otherwise, be lent, re-sold, hired out, or otherwise circulated without the publisher's prior consent in any form of binding or cover other than that which it is published and without a similar condition including this condition being imposed on the subsequent purchaser.

In this work of fiction, the characters, places and events are either the product of the author's imagination or they are used entirely fictitiously. Any resemblance to actual persons, living or dead, is purely coincidental.

Swirl is an imprint of arima publishing.

arima publishing
ASK House, Northgate Avenue
Bury St Edmunds, Suffolk IP32 6BB
t: (+44) 01284 700321

www.arimapublishing.com

af @ quantumchronicles.com

Anthony was born in London on the 6th of January 1975, from Italian parents. He was training to become a professional footballer in Spain with Atletico Marbella, and also had various trials around Europe. He studied Theology and Philosophy, and also entered the field of Engineering, becoming an ROV Pilot. Anthony is now a Science Fiction writer. His books consist of short stories containing elements of Philosophy and Theology.

www. quantumchronicles. com

CONTENTS

Introduction

Quantum Chronicles 2 is a book comprised of 13 Sci-Fi tales, each one with a flair and theme of its own, leaving the reader with a compelling message and twist......

The very first story I wrote was 'Destination Citon', a tale which appears later in the book. The main theme to this one is 'What is reality?' Does the mind construct reality? How much of what we call reality is actually real?

After a time of much reflection, I was inexorably compelled to choose my first story for the book, 'At Your Request'. This is a tale that leaves us with a profound philosophical question, an essential question, one that we may have failed to tackle, but one that demands an answer if we are to be certain of ourselves and our place in this amazing world... 'What is it to be human?' Is it the planet we are born on? Is it our appearance, our mind, that has the neurological capacity to create wonders, or is there something far deeper and more significant that lies within each one of us; Perhaps something a finely tuned robot is devoid of, along with the animal kingdom, which coexists around us?

This is the question I leave you with, in the hope that you find an answer. Perhaps in it lies the key to life....the very key to our existence.....

God bless......

13 SCI-FI TALES

Man is held within the sphere of time and Space...
but beyond it lies another realm....

At Your Request
William Leadholm, widower, on the verge of suicide, heads to Earth, where he can have his late wife reconstructed to his exact specifications

The Memory of Green
Sean Winters, lunar resident, pursues a lifetime dream when he travels to Earth. With limited time he sets out to unfold its mysteries

The Man Who Awoke Yesterday
Dirk Allen awakens in unfamiliar surroundings and soon faces a brutal reality as his very own existence is now called into question

Slit in the Sky
Crazed Scientist, Eric Western, manufacturer of the T-Propeller, is on a quest to prove that all life on earth originated from aliens

The Appointment
The planet Orious sits uniquely in deep space....Ludovic Martel, Terra Ambassador, meets with its leader with an unexpected message

The Hidden Cave
Deep beneath the sea lies a doorway into a parallel dimension.....Cliff Fontaine soon discovers this when his world is turned upside down. Is there a way back?

Terra Unknown
Commander Myers arrives on an unknown planet, one far out in another solar system where nothing but the relics of a past existence remains

Destination Citon
Imagine waking up and discovering your whole life has been manufactured

11

Spy Hunter
Beyond the confines of a subterranean world, mutants stalk the surface of the radioactive earth with an unwanted guest

Mind Blitz
In a world where your thoughts and ideas are no longer your own, people who set out to conceal them are deemed evil

Memoirs of Time
Boris Muller finds the key to unlock the gateway of time

He Dreams Planet Earth
Mind Control: the ultimate crime prevention

The Edge of Eternity
At death what happens to that invisible energy of the brain known as consciousness?

At Your Request

Down a steel state highway, William Leadholm sat in a surface-cab, contemplating the babble of his own thoughts as they echoed through his mind. Ahead a vast panorama stretched, a sun-shimmering metropolis now slowly coming into view as the robot driver increased velocity.

"*How far to go..?*" William exclaimed in an unsteady nervous tone, cigarette between his teeth.

The robot referred to the time distance indicator across the gleaming control board:

"*Five scheduled minutes......*"

In no time, the surface-cab arrived, halting smoothly. Pressing his hand against the credit register, William stepped out dashing towards a grey-domed building. Reading the luminous indication map he made his way up the stairs, two at a time. He vaguely recalled the way, even though a year had passed. Then he caught sight of the flashing arrowed sign, '*Love Reunited.*' Throwing his weight against the heavy white door, he entered the main reception. Robot workers and humans filled the lobby going about their daily activities. In the last two years, Earth had become a planet infested with machines; statistically there were more robots than humans. With his sole objective in mind, he gazed around, almost dismissing the scene.

Suddenly, a robot nurse came over towards him holding a tray of metallic components. A name lay across the bundle, '*Mrs S. Jones.*' He loosened his collar, licking his lips. '*Cindy would be nothing more than that pile of metal she was holding,*' he thought introspectively. The robot now stood face to face with him shaking her head, her photocell eyes narrowing down his image.

"*No smoking Sir.....See the sign?*"

"*I'm sorry, just a little anxious.*"

Across both cheeks, two spots of red glowed. He swallowed hard, dropping his cigarette to the floor, stamping on it with his heel.

"*Are you here to see someone?*"

"*Yes, yes, I am.....Doctor Nash. I'm five minutes late already.*"

His anxiety was building up, manifested in his posture, voice, and trembling hands.

"*Down the hall to your right...at the far end, you can't miss it.*"

Pushing on with tunnel-like vision, he pierced through the endless tide of activity. Nothing could deflect him from his long awaited moment which had now arrived. Reaching the door, it opened mechanically.

"*Mr Leadholm, please enter,*" a calm sophisticated voice spoke.

He stepped in battling with his emotions. His heartbeat began to increase. Sitting in a chair was the doctor dressed in a dark blue suit, a highly advanced robot constructed in humanoid form. He had the physical appearance of a man right down to the last detail, with an intellectual insight and faculty way beyond that of a human being, unlike the other finely assembled metallic workers. He was slim with refined features, his eyes dark green, his cheeks freckled, but something about his voice was peculiar, the one flaw in such a perfect construction.

"*It's been quite a while, a year to the day......How was your trip from Krutopa....Still busy building the new space station there I take it?*"

"*Not me,*"....William replied, his voice full of conceit. "*My five hundred workers....*"

"*Yes, yes, that's right, how foolish of me. Time does have such a terrible effect on memory......You're the Technical Director aren't you?*"

"*Doc, please, I can't wait anymore....*"

"*Patience....relax...she's ready for you....*"

"*Where is it then......?*"

"*It.....?*"

"*Well, it is a robot, is it not? ......Just like you, just like all of you......*" He clenched his fists, dots of sweat surfacing across his forehead.

"*Come now, Mr Leadholm, what's gotten into you?*"

The Doctor stood up, walked over to him, guiding him into the seat in front of the desk. William held his head to the floor glaring down sullenly.

"*It appears to me you are still very confused, neurotic, very emotionally unbalanced.... I hope you are ready for this.....*"

He sat crossing his legs, regarding him with sharp eyed perspicacity.

"*Are you?*"

There was a moment of penetrating silence......

"*As you know, at this agency we place emphasis on psychological release with all our clients. It appears you're still suffering from periodic bouts of depression. You've had a whole year of therapy back on Krutopa......*"

He paused.

"*Remember it's all a question of psychology, cognitive psychology, conditioning of the mind. Clearly your view of robots is still distorted and negative, but regardless of that, if you believe she's real, real she is. Objectively maybe not, but who cares what most humans think...? It's a subjective approach that counts. If she is real to you nothing else should matter.*"

The doctor sat back tilting his chair...convinced of his own existence....convinced he too was alive and real.

"*Mr Leadholm, I suggest that you don't philosophise too much, it will do you no good. Trust me, in a month or so you won't even recall this discussion...besides, legally, she's alive.*"

The words reverberated around the room......

"*Does it know......sorry, she.....?*" William asked flatly.

"*Know what?*"

"*That she's a robot...?*"

"*How could she not know what she is? Aesthetically she's as human as can be, identical to your late wife Cindy both in appearance and character......even her voice has been modified to that of your wife. The air compressed voice disc is very special.*"

'*Too bad yours isn't,*' William thought cynically.

"*Tell me Doc, will she really have the same characteristics...I mean in every way?*"

"*Yes Sir, just as you requested.....kind and sweet with all the other qualities Cindy had....minus the negatives of course....*"

William grinned, the words thundering in his ears.

"*She will not nag and whine, or give conflicting orders, she will be submissive at all times...an altruist, a giver in all ways......*"

"*What about her memory......all the ones I shared with Cindy?*"

"*She will have none. Although she knows who you are her husband, she will be devoid of all the memories you and Cindy shared. It's a complete new start. She will need to learn about you, her home, etc. Teach her the ways, share your experiences. A fresh new chapter awaits you both. "*

"*Will she die?*"

"*Everything ceases to be Mr Leadholm, biological or mechanical, it's the cycle of life......The universal law......Nothing can stand against the force of time.....*"

"*But......but she must have a basic life expectancy....*"

"*Of course, sixty years of longevity, beyond that point she will cease to be. Considering you're thirty-six, she should outlive you. The other plus is that she will never have to experience that awful decaying process that all you humans go through......ageing. But anyway this is all academic...Above all she will love you, unconditionally..."*

"*Really......?*" William muttered. His eyes lit with anticipation.

"*Yes, really Sir......I've spoken and examined her meticulously....she's a wonderful woman, highly intelligent, very engaging....but you need to give her time to mould....adjust into the world, especially on Krutopa, so please be patient..."*

"*You know Doc, it isn't easy when you've lost someone you love....Death is hard to take, especially after six years of marriage....I was close to ending my life....had it not been for..."*

"*Us....?* "*Love Reunited....?*" You can put all those painful memories aside. You came to us a year ago, the only legalised planet in the entire galaxy to indulge in such a practice......travelled fifty-eight thousand light years to Earth, as you have now, in order to get back the woman you love...Well, she's ready for you...."*

William let his breath out in weightless relief......

"*Just as well there are no laws prohibiting her living on Krutopa...."*

The doctor smiled, tapping his fingers on the glazed desk top.

"*Before we go any further, there are a few routine documents that you have to sign and fill out.*"

From a drawer, he produced the relevant papers, with it a pen.

"*If you would please...."*

Hurriedly, William read through, almost dismissively, nervously filling out each section. He just wanted to see her......it!

"*Okay Doc, all done......*"

He shifted the pile over, dropping the pen on top. He had regained strength and mental equilibrium, evident by the gleam in his eyes. The Doctor flipped rapidly through the sheets, analysing. His photocell brain span operating at high velocity, relays and memory banks clicked. Switches activated internally, allowing a surge of electricity to flow.

"*Okay Mr Leadholm....you've waited long enough.*"

The wall behind the doctor faded, turning from a white solid concrete block to transparent. They were now looking into a brightly lit room. There was motion and sound, faint but definite. William watched on critically, his heartbeat increasing. He felt slightly faint. With a hum the walls parted from the centre point, like an opening curtain. There, standing before them was Cindy, dressed in a white medical robe, a robot technician by her side. The Doctor motioned them forward. William rose, mouth gaping. She was perfect, identical to the very inch. Her face was well chiselled and pale, velvety-like skin, her eyes cold blue, hair dark brown, almost black; her feet petite and sculptured.

"*Cindy......Cindy....*"

He raced over and held her, squeezing her with emotion, years of pain and heartache. She was warm and substantial, her white robe rustling as she moved against him.

"*William, Oh William....*" She looked into his eyes dreamily, breathless and excited. "*We have so much to see...so much to do....*"

Her supple arms circled his neck, her red lips delicate and moist.

"*Yes sweetheart......now that we are together I'm complete, you have given me a reason to live....Come......we have two days left here.....Friday we leave for Krutopa.....*"

"*Krutopa......how faraway is it?*" she replied, letting the word roll and spin around her mechanical brain.

"*Fifty-eight thousand light years away....in another region of this galaxy....miraculously discovered seventy years back...a clean beautiful virgin land, with an ocean...eroded cliffs and mountains...forests, rivers and waterfalls....landscapes, the magnificence of which you couldn't imagine. There are many colonists there, families from all over the galaxy......*"

Her eyes sparkled with excitement, an inner innocence. The doctor pulled the blinds eradicating the sunlight which had now filtered through. The room sank into an amber glow. William pulled away from her gently, stepping towards the doctor.

"*Thank you*"......he said, peering over his shoulder at his lovely Cindy. "*I don't know what to say...*"

He blushed, his face contorted with emotion, pulled out of its natural form by inner forces and feelings.

"*Mr Leadholm, remember......this all happened because of you....it was done at your request...*"

The doctor signalled to the robot technician. He turned, holding Cindy by the hand, walking her back inside the room, silent and efficient. With a thump the wall transformed back into a solid white concrete block.

"*Hey, where's she going..?*"

"*Patience Sir....she needs to be dressed....she'll be with you in around five minutes....*"

The doctor smiled warmly, rubbing his hands with satisfaction. Task accomplished. It was complete. An overwhelming feeling of achievement tingled through his body, electrically induced. There was a knock, a metallic head popped around the door as it opened...

"*Doctor Nash.....I've got a Mr Watson in reception, a human...he's pretty bad...*"

"*Okay nurse, see him through...*"

"*Well....that's that, I guess,*" William said excitedly...

"*Remember Mr Leadholm....in a year's time, you are scheduled to return......a relationship check up if you like......*

A one off...but it's paramount. Now if you wouldn't mind waiting in reception, I have another client......"

He tapped his wrist at his vid-watch. Perceiving the hint William turned for the door.

"*Thanks Doc...thanks for everything....*"

Stepping out into the world of commotion and activity, William took in a breath of fresh air, Cindy close by, warm sunlight streaming down on them. Gazing ahead, they digested the scene...... The huge rumbling city of Los Angeles was crammed with people moving along the streets, chatting, walking into shops, bars, parks and buildings. Surface vehicles filled the roads buzzing by, interplanetary-jets moving above in the atmosphere, flashing projectiles of metal in suspension and blistering motion. A section of the city rose high, skyscrapers piercing into the clouds. A hover-train-track encircled it, disappearing into the distance, signal lights flickering dimly at brief calculated intervals. Cindy's eyes roamed like a lost child, getting to grips with the complex tangle and confusion of the world.

"*Wow.....the city is beautiful.....isn't it?*"

"*Yes sweetheart, it is indeed......*"

They walked on leisurely, strolling hand in hand like two juveniles, gripped in teenage love. Then, from the corner of his eye, William spotted a cab. Waving it down, it drew up instantly beside the curb.

"*Where to....?*" the robot driver inquired.....

"*Aphrodite Hotel...*"

Jumping in, the surface-cab zipped off turning a corner, spiralling cautiously towards the underground highway......

In the dim amber light of the hotel bar, William and Cindy sat, eyes fixed on each other intently, a shared hungry look. The bar was located undersea, the only section of the hotel sub-aqua. The ambience was warm, soft, alternating lights flickering across the floor and beautifully sculptured ceiling. It resembled an ancient Greek temple. In the background music played, instrumental with a mystical Arabian beat.

"*Waiter......*" William signalled, catching view of the dense pacific waters which engulfed them in the circular structured bar. For a brief moment he saw a large fish through the glass. The robot waitress now approached.

"*Yes Sir, what can I get you?*" She held the com-board expertly waiting for the order.

"*Two chocolate flavoured coffees...*"

He looked over at Cindy, smiling, recalling; awakening renewed emotion in him.

"*Extra cream in one please...*" he murmured dreamily...

William leaned towards her, his elbow resting against the table which diffused a pale green light. It spread over his features.....

"*You always loved it that way.....*"

He smiled to himself, lost temporarily in nostalgic thought. Memories. There was no response from her, other than a bashful smile.

"*Tell me William......tell me about yourself....*"

"*What do you want to know...?*"

"*Anything......everything...*"

She reached over, holding his hand, her nails well manicured and exquisitely tapered, eyes glowing with interest.

"*Back home I'm the Technical Director of a construction company......we build apartments......houses, even space stations. We're currently working on one...it will be the fourth on the planet....it's massive....*"

"*What about the planet itself, Krutopa? Is it similar to here in terms of way of life......?*"

"*Every planet has to keep pace....*"

"*With......?*"

"*With the general trend of the galactic culture, which was formulated here on Earth, the central source....but yes of course...there are some inevitable differences.....legal ones for sure.....*"

Abruptly, the robot waitress placed the tray of coffees on the table, severing the flow of the conversation. *'Damn robots,'* he thought, *'no matter how sophisticated they were they simply lacked that human touch....'* Ironically, overwhelmed by passion, he had almost forgotten that Cindy was inorganic.....

"If you would, please Sir......"

He pressed his finger against the credit register. The tiny device clicked and flashed.

"Thank you......enjoy."

"I'm sorry, where was I?" he said, moving the tray into the centre of the table.

"Have you travelled much....? I mean in this solar system..."

She lifted the mug of choc-coffee, taking a few cautious sips.

"Yes as a matter of fact, I have...."

For a moment he paused....taken over by flickering waves of emotion......

"I was on Mars several times after they melted the ice caps.

Interestingly the distance between Earth and Mars is variable, due to their elliptical orbits around the sun......The gravity is much weaker on Mars, never liked it though......nothing going, just mountains, a few bars and restaurants, lots of construction, and the locals were very grumpy....."

"Anywhere else....?" She licked her lips, the froth melting away into liquid.

"The moon, Lunar......it's close by, Earth's only natural satellite..."

"Wow...."

"Unfortunately most of the planets in this system are uninhabitable...that's why I've always hated it here....Venus is volcanic...just lava and steam, way too hot......As for the gigantic planets like Jupiter and Saturn, they are nothing but giant balls of gas without a conventional solid surface. Besides, you would be crushed on entry....and to date no known metal could withstand such pressure...."

In the brief silence that followed, William was caught, hypnotised by her beauty. It was surreal; everything about her was identical to his wife, the posture, the look, the slight motion of her body.

"What's Lunar like?" she asked, breaking his stunned gaze.

"Lunar......?"

He raised his hands expressively, masking his feelings.

"An indoor existence......huge oxygen pumped cities. In general the people there are a lot taller and thinner, as a result of the moon's weak gravitational field. Environment and gravity play a key role in how humans evolve physically....genetically."

Her face lit with enthusiasm as the information filtered through.

"I see that my experiences fascinate you...." His voice was faint but passionate. She blushed. Her eyes sparkled, alive with emotion.

"How long were you there..?"

"Two months. I worked there during college break...needed the extra cash....good rates...I guess that's why I eventually left Earth..."

She leaned back crossing her legs. A cloud of cigarette smoke drifted by, sucked automatically towards the fume detector across the ceiling greedily.

"Here you spend most of your life working for just a few credits......The virgin planets in contrast pay well...handsomely, that's why very few humans now remain here......Most live on Andradome."

"Andradome...?"

"It's in my solar system, furthest one out....I've been there...it's pretty rough, annual periodic meteor swarms....constant bad weather...but plenty of unlimited opportunities...it's even being nicknamed the golden globe......"

"Was it always like that..?"

"No, it took time for it to develop....time before a rational working system was implemented. Originally the locals were very withdrawn, almost tribal, a decentralized society locked into their own way of thinking....the best way..."

His eyes rolled sardonically....

"I guess it's because they are so far out.....cut off a little...It was a society that initially rejected the advanced technocratic and cultural commodities of the galaxy. Even now some still want independence.....took years before the government signed the U.G.C Articles....."

He cut off sharply....

"I'm probably boring you, right? I'm sorry....I guess I'm so taken aback by everything....Usually when I'm nervous I rattle on....get lost in my own world......was like that as a kid...."

"You're not boring me......nothing you say or do, could ever...."

"But surely you must have certain likes and dislikes...don't you..?"

"Your desires are my desires.....your dreams are my dreams..."

The reality of her nature, once again penetrated. William fought it, regaining composure. She reached over and held his hand mesmerised, gazing at him profoundly. Both of them smiled; a smile of complete understanding.

"Tell me, will it take long to reach Krutopa?"

"No it's very quick. Once we've ascended into a point in space......we enter a wormhole.....it's basically a shortcut through space and time.....Wormholes allow you to travel from one point of the universe to another in an instant....that's how we reach planets light years away. Our galaxy, the Milky Way is enormous you know......approximately one hundred thousand light years in diameter......"

"What did you study in college? You appear to have quite an intellect."

"Come on.....it's basic stuff..."

She chuckled in amusement...

"I studied engineering....but I always loved philosophy, metaphysics....I dabbled in a bit here and there.....theories of ultimate reality......purpose of life......"

"You know, William....we are going to be so happy together......"

Her eyelashes flickered modestly, her chiselled face well marked out in the dim light.

"I love you more than anything.....more than life....this is meant to be......"

Overcome, and for a brief moment, all he could see were her lips moving, no sound coming at all, eradicated by languid dream-like thoughts which rippled through his mind.

"Yes Cindy......I've always loved you...things are going to be just perfect......this is only the beginning....."

A year had elapsed......

"Err, Doctor Nash.....you have a client waiting in your office. Apparently he is quite upset, very agitated....his file is on your desk......"

"Thank you nurse......"

Doctor Nash walked in and studied his client intuitively. Relays and memory banks clicked......a selection of possible image comparisons buzzing through his mechanical mind.

"Yes that's it, Mr Leadholm......I recall you....I, do beg your pardon......I see many clients from all over...you're the gentleman from Krutopa...we last met......"

"*A year to the day,*" William said piercingly, controlling his emotions with effort.

"*That's right, here for your review...let me refresh my memory.*"

Promptly, he flicked through the file absorbing the data, his eyes scanning....lips twitching. William sat there motionless,

...his features distorted with irritation. He appeared withdrawn, drained of life and energy.

"*So......how have things progressed with you?*" The doctor consulted his vid-watch, pushing back his shirt sleeve. "*How are things with Mrs Leadholm? I take it all is not well...*"

William dabbed his forehead with a hanky, shifted around on his chair a few times in a series of nervous motions and then replied.

"*Not so good Doctor Nash......not good at all...*"

The doctor frowned.....almost shocked...

"*Really, why......? She loves you....does she not..?*"

"*Oh yes......there's no doubt about that......*"

"*Well......what's the problem then?*" He raised both hands.

"*Just that....*"

"*Just what Mr Leadholm....?*" The pitch in his voice rose.

"*Doctor, it isn't real......*"

"*It......! We've discussed this already......Remember it's a question of psychology....*"

"*It hasn't even adjusted to the human scent...*"

"*Mr Leadholm.....it took me sometime to......*"

William's eyes grew wide with cold twisting fury.

"*You're ignoring reality Doctor.....humans and machines are totally different, a maze of wires cannot replace a beating heart......I've acquired a pet....nothing more than a pet, even then, most are disobedient....She just follows and agrees with ...everything I say and do....she has no personality of her own....none whatsoever....there is a distinct bias in everything she says and does in order to fit into my line of thinking.....*"

"*And....? You wanted unconditional love did you not?*"

"*That isn't it.....Cindy doesn't love......it has no sense of the actual meaning. Real love, natural love is something else. She's programmed, an artificial life source, imitating a far superior life form. Her love, her sentiments are nothing but programs......electrical signals whizzing around her, through her so that she corresponds* to certain actions and emotions......she isn't human, Doctor Nash......she's a machine...a highly advanced machine...."

"*Sir*"....He banged his fist against the glazed desk sending a few sheets of paper drifting to the ground....

"*As a humanoid I take offence...that distortion you have lodged in your mind hasn't seemed to have left you...You came here with one objective......*"

Slowly he began to regain composure....

"*We fulfilled our task......we gave her to you real or not, and worked frantically around your specifications......If it is true love you're in search of....human love as you call it, well I'm afraid that is out of my jurisdiction......*"

"*True love*," William muttered under his breath.... "*Human love....it's biological, it stems from the soul, it lies deep within us, within the very fabric of man......It's an abstract emotion.....displayed by actions...deeds.....it can't be bought or manufactured.....it's something that no machine can mimic......it's a very special gift......*"

"*Indeed, Mr Leadholm......indeed......but what is it to be human? What is it to be alive? Whether programmed or not she acts, responds, does, says, loves....who cares how those feelings and emotions are induced or generated....who's to say*

...that you as a human are not somehow programmed yourself......?"

He cut off emphatically, and at once the silence penetrated.

"*I think that'll be all*," William said, getting to his feet. "*Nothing can bring her back......perhaps in time the scars will heal...perhaps not.....*"

"*Time Mr Leadholm, time will indeed be your only friend, in these circumstances at least, but then again, there are some things in time that will never erode....or indeed be forgotten......*"

The Memory of Green

Accelerating to its maximum velocity, T-11 ascended towards the darkness of space, its lights flashing like fire, sweeping across the lunar surface. Gaining prompt altitude, the face of the globe grew smaller, the space-station disappearing, fading into a meaningless speck. Through vocal activation, Sean flicked by the various channels in search of entertainment. *'Mundane and boring,'* he thought until channel 7 captured his attention. Before his eyes, narrated by the ubiquitous Professor Kepplar was a virtual space tour. An unknown planet suddenly revolved around the screen, one which was located in a different region of galaxy. The image then magnified, displaying its lifeless, sun baked steaming volcanic landscape. Fiddling with the aud-dial, he looked on with growing interest. *'Fascinating,'* he muttered under his breath until the image began to slowly fade. Wave interference......blank.

"*Miss....oh miss....*" he rasped, waving his arm to acquire the attention of the blond airhostess, who instantly acknowledged his signal. Having duly caught her attention, he lowered his arm, eyes full of expectancy......

"*How can I help Sir?*"

Against the grey of her jacket, he noticed her name in bold white letters.

"*Sandrine, there's no transmission......*" He indicated the blank screen with a sweep of his hand.

"*Sorry Sir, it does occur regularly......As we leave the moon's gravitational field there are sometimes minor problems with the entertainment broadcasting signal, give it a few minutes......*"

Smiling brightly she turned, making her way down the aisle of the ship, appeasing the other passengers with her sensitive attention. Dismissing the matter, Sean glanced through the side-window, his destination in mind. Far out in the distance, he caught sight of it; the blue rotating sphere, Earth, as he had done from his lunar-base countless times before. It hung there, frozen in time like a striking precious jewel, enclosed in its own blue bubble of atmosphere and activity, manufacturing, breathing its own oxygen. *'Blue,'* he thought, *'a vast ocean, an endless expanse of water.....life.'* This excited him. He recalled the images he had seen via powerful telescope, the sun shimmering, dancing across the cold waters of the Pacific and Atlantic. With a nervous hand, he adjusted the flow of oxygen, twisting a dial above his head, gripped by both fear and wonder; two conflicting emotions.

Time stretched, an hour passed. T-11 now assumed an orbit outside the gravity belt of the planet, a blazing mass of white lighting the trackless void......

In the Customs lounge of the New York State space-station, Sean walked through, bag in hand, his green attire blending in with the other lunar passengers. The station itself was filled with luminous pillars, positioned mathematically in all directions in order to maintain and support the alloys which evidently made up the structure. Gazing around like a lost child in search of direction, he felt lonely and fearful, yet his surging curiosity was enough to quench and nullify those impeding emotions which threatened to overwhelm him. After years of pent up desire, he had finally come to the place, the place where earthly reality had been nothing more than a dream, until now.

Approaching the Check-Port, Sean held out his hand. A small metallic machine stood there functioning homeostatically, orienting itself under human supervision. It would roll slightly forward then backwards on its four metal wheels, registering passenger by passenger, supplying itself with the necessary data. On the odd occasion it would bleep, indicating no admission. The cycle repeated itself in rhythmic motion. It was now Sean's turn.

"*Next,*" a security guard mumbled......

With his hand raised, he aligned himself with the machine, marked out by a yellow line across the floor. The cycle at once commenced. From a tiny aperture, it emitted a wink of red light as it began to roll forward. Its trajectory was spot on as it met with his coded hand, depositing his information as a permanent record within its rapidly operating complex system.

Now, slightly aggravated, he passed under an arc screen, phase two of the monitoring process; a DNA data collector. In a fraction of a second it removed a hair follicle from his scalp, storing it accordingly.

The exit now came into view as he looked ahead through towering glass doors. He could see people, earth people massed together in chaos and confusion, clothed in a variety of colours, something which the lunar residents were not accustomed to. How he wished he had someone waiting for him. It was just him alone, alone to face the untamed world of earthly existence. His relatives spoke continually of its beauty, but also of its danger and ugliness. He recalled the words of his grandfather, '*Sean, Earth is a jungle like no other, the animals who dwell in their own, live and act on predatory instinct, but Man, earthly Man is a cocktail of unpredictability's, good and evil, highs and lows, their behavioural patterns constantly altering in untimely sporadic bursts. Unlike an animal, the duality of man is unique.*' He smiled, recapturing the moment fully; he could almost picture his grandfather as if it were the other day, mumbling these words at the lunar base. With the clenching of a fist, as if to transmit courage into himself, he muttered, '*I will blend in, I will get to grips with this world......surely.*'

Stepping out of the space-station, into the open atmosphere, he took in his first deep breath of air. It felt good, his nostrils flaring as he inhaled again. Instantly he detected the scent of flowers commingling with the foul odours of the city. He smiled, looking into the blue, gazing at the sun, its heat and radiance penetrating into his depths warming him inwardly, an experience that he had been devoid of. '*Lunar was radically different,*' he thought, making sharp, brief comparisons in his jaded mind. Up above, life was an enclosed existence, fuelled by canned oxygen which was perpetually pumped into the lunar structures. Beyond the confines of the indoor world, it was lifeless, bleak and hostile, a globe without atmosphere due to its small mass and consequently insufficient gravitational field. A landscape filled with gaping craters formed by explosive impacts of high velocity asteroids......comets. Adjusting to the Earth's gravity was only going to be a minor problem; after all, the lunar cities simulated Earth-like gravity was almost exact.

Gripped in awe, he walked onto a patch of muddy soil gazing at a tiny spider. He pointed and laughed, amazed by what he saw, recalling his brief lessons in entomology. Kneeling, he placed his hand by it, surveying its motion; it moved, dancing around his fingers in search of refuge, perhaps seeking a path to freedom. Having dutifully accomplished the task, thus quenching his longing desire, he flung it onto the soil below; watching it disappear into a jungle of grass and weeds. He paused for a time, pensive yet alert.

Standing, he made an imprint, pressing down hard on the mud. As child-like as it was, he felt the urge to make his mark on the new world which his ancestors spoke of so highly. *'My first time on Earth,'* he thought jubilantly, *'perhaps the last....'* Knowing he had only a week, as Earth legislation permitted, he wanted to make the most of his experience. It would be another year before he could make the next trip. A deafening beep distracted him, dissolving his thoughts in an instant. He turned, gazing at a row of sky-cabs, the drivers in their matching blue uniforms and hats perspiring in the humidity of the day. Suddenly, a large group of tourists appeared, rushing out of the station, lugging bulky cases, rapidly dispersing in all directions.

Fishing deep inside his pockets with anxious hands, he pulled out his accommodation voucher, the one that came with the package deal. Small glossy and polished, it reflected the sunlight into his left eye. Across the voucher imprinted in black, were the words, *'Welcome to Earth...'*

After a smooth brisk air journey the cab manoeuvred for descent, landing outside the Volux Hotel, its ten star sign flashing and revolving every four seconds sequentially. Raising his hand before the code reader, the driver said, correctly, stiffly, *"You're a Lunar resident aren't you......?"*

"Yes indeed I am.....How did you perceive that? My clothes, no doubt......"

The driver pointed to the small credit screen.

"No Earth resident gets charged that kind of tariff...Have a good day Sir...."

Sean acknowledged the amount with disinterest, quickly shifting his glance towards the towering hotel. The cab door, via automatic control, slid open, concealing itself within its shell. He stepped out, regulating the temperature of his suit, his bag hanging across his shoulder loosely. Again he refocused and was taken aback by its stupendous design. It had the flair of an ancient Greek monument, carved and shaped to precision; an echo of the past. As he entered through the parting glass doors, a porter walked over.

"Welcome to the Volux Hotel. Please make your way to reception......"

Sean commenced a slow walk over, and in the background captured muffled notes of hostility. People turned staring, hard and cold, child and adult alike. Their transparent resentment induced feelings of inadequacy within him, as if he were an invader from another world passing the outer limits. Accommodating himself to the ever growing intimidating atmosphere, he reached the well lit reception desk....

"Hello Sir," a tall green eyed lady said, her words spaced apart, her Russian accent dominant and penetrating.

"You're from Lunar aren't you Mr Winters?" She smiled, a smile that lit up her Slavic features, even teeth sparkling white under the intense overhead light.

"Yes, yes I am......how did you know my name...?"

"We have a tracking device implanted in the wall above. Within seconds it picks up all your data from your coded hand....displaying it across my com-screen..."

He grinned rubbing his chin.

"Tell me Mr Winters, I've always wondered what it must be like up there on the Moon....haven't saved enough to get a flight yet. At night I often sit back and watch it....the near side of course....because of the Moon's synchronous rotation the far side is never visible......"

"It's interesting...a totally different world even though so near. Sometimes it's the places closest to us that we take for granted....Man has a tendency to look afar. For an earth citizen it would be hard to adjust to a radically different social order......"

Absorbed in his words for a time, she spoke. *"I remember as a child seeing ships departing for Lunar on the vision-set."* Her eyes now semi-closed, became distant as she reflected..."*They would takeoff, leaving Terra, voyaging into space.....lining up with the Moon, falling into an orbit around it a hundred miles above its surface, guided down by magnetic controls......but of course with anti-gravity technology it's all changed, if you can afford it......"*

Swiftly he replied, somewhat startled by her baffling fount of knowledge.

"You seem pretty clued up for a receptionist....sounds like you are speaking from personal experience...."

"My dad was a Project Manager......he designed most of the ships for Lunar Voyagers....he would always go on about it......"

With a warm waving motion of her hand, she now signalled over to a porter.

"You're all done Mr Winters...."

"That's it....?"

"Yes Sir......the machine above has obtained a photographic record of all your data, checking you in.....In terms of gaining access into your room....simply pass your hand by the small blue code beam beside the door...."

"Great, thanks......"

Directed by the porter, he was led to his room on the fortieth floor. Beside the door Sean flung his hand at the code beam. Magnetic locks instantly gave, slipping out of place. Then with a sharp click the door opened, swinging aside.

"*Will that be all Mr Winters......?*"

"*Yes.....thank you......*"

"*Sir, before I forget, we have a new service available for all our outer space guests...it's only just come in......*"

"*Oh yeah....?*" Sean exclaimed attentively.

"*It's a Virtual Chamber.....In a few hours you can travel and see the world and all its beauty as if you were really there......you won't know the difference...*"

"*Really......?*"

"*Yes Sir it's a very special machine,*" he said coaxingly. "*If you require more information just dial 8 from your vid-phone, you'll be put straight through......*"

Sean entered the room, its colour-alternating walls faintly luminous. Against the glass frame on a hanging picture, an angry fly buzzed. Dropping his bag onto the floor he walked over to the balcony, the doors sliding apart as the heat sensors registered. He stepped out stretching, gazing at the sun as it hung high above the face of the Atlantic. Then an intercity cruiser shot past, leaving a slash of billowing smoke in the atmosphere. Suddenly a thought struck him. '*This chamber; what was behind such a mechanism, how could it create such an illusion?*' A devouring curiosity grew within him. He stopped his introspection, and headed inside. Now, beside the vid-phone, he dialled 8, acquiring immediate connection...

"*For visual transmission, press 1, if not please hold.....*"

He refrained, opting for only sound. After a sequence of beeps a blade sharp voice spoke......

"*Erica Holmes, how can I assist you?*"

"*Yes hi, I'm interested in this Virtual Chamber......*"

"*Oh yes, Sir,*" she replied brightly, "*It's the latest machine, the very finest technology......At your own discretion and speed you can visit the world, all four corners of it...an experience of a lifetime....The procedure is simple, via vocal activation you can be anywhere you choose....and I mean anywhere.....Asia, Africa, Europe.....your choice.*"

There was a brief interval of silence.

"You see Sir, travelling with the Virtual Chamber is safer and easier, not to mention cost effective......Just think, in the legal week that you have as a Lunar resident you could never see the world in its entirety......not to mention the amount of credits you would have to spend......but with the Virtual Chamber you can accomplish your wildest dreams within a matter of hours...."

He interjected.

"How real does it feel, I mean I was told it's as if I were really there?"

"Yes Sir that's correct....your conscious mind won't know the difference, you will feel and see everything as if you were really there......as if you were part of that existence, that reality......One minute you'll be strolling through the city of Cairo, the next trudging through the jungles of Africa......it really is something phenomenal......"

His face lit up with exuberance......pictures forming, weaving through his mind....The lady continued....

"And you can benefit further from the experience."

"How, in what way......?"

"Photos can be included with the package to add verisimilitude to the journey, an extra touch of reality..."

"Okay, so what's the total cost?" Sean inquired, his voice momentarily losing its spark.

"Eight hundred credits for an eight hour journey.....that's with everything included..."

"Done," he said nodding in agreement, his expression set and assured.

"Great, as you are a guest, the V Chamber is available for you this evening. It operates on a twenty four hour basis......seven days a week.....and for your information, you are advised to stay away from alcohol."

"Tell me, what section of the hotel are you located in?"

He tapped his mouth with his fingers gently.

"Level thirty...and if you require further information, just select X across your vision-set, it will give you a scientific breakdown of its function, and will answer any niggling questions you may feel are of importance."

With a click, the call ended. Then, through a thin opening across the vid-phone unit, a note slithered out face down. Snatching it, he read......

"Thank you for your call Mr Winters, the Volux Hotel wishes you a pleasant stay...."

Sean sat across the bed, swiftly assimilating all the information. If only Lunar could have these machines it would save so much credit and time, but in retrospect he knew it would never happen. The government would never implement the necessary legislation for the acquisition of such a machine. Solar travel would die.....Lunar depended on it. He began to recollect the words which played in his mind... *'With the Virtual Chamber you can accomplish your wildest dreams'......* *'Dreams being the operative word,'* he thought bitterly. After all, however authentic it felt, virtual it remained, at least objectively. *'No matter what, the machine could never compare to the real thing,'* he concluded. In his mind it remained an ignominious option, but in the prevailing circumstances, a good one.

Striding into the bathroom lithely, he filled the sink with tepid water, splashing it across his face and neck. Although clearly exhausted, and in need of sleep the excitement of the moment kept him sharp and alert. He was filled with gleeful anticipation, unable to rest. Drying himself with a warm towel, he looked into the mirror, wondering what awaited him.

As evening approached, Sean walked out of the glass hover-lift, gazing back at the Moon nostalgically with a sense of awe. It was the first time he had seen it from another world, hanging there, suspended in the far off distance, frozen in deep space, foggy webs of moisture drifting across its face. Memories flooded his mind......he recalled the times he would sit staring at the Earth from Lunar, wondering, thinking about the affinity between the two. After all, the Moon was responsible for most of the tidal effects seen on the Earth. Shrugging his shoulders, the metal lift doors closed, killing off the scene.

Strolling down a long twisting hallway, luxury suites either side, he saw a flashing green sign. It read, *'V CHAMBER...GLOBAL TOUR.'* In the background, he detected the enchanting chords of Far Eastern music, dimly echoing. As he reached the end of the hall, a vertically lifting door opened before him. He stepped in. Sean's attention was immediately drawn to a jet black machine, its large frame occupying most of the space around the room. The V Chamber! It certainly resembled the images he had seen on the vision-set, but in reality it had more to it, much more. It was spherical in shape, yet its middle section extended out, swollen, as if a ring had been placed around it.

Suddenly, he was approached by a tall athletic looking man, with short blond hair. Using his anthropological knowledge, Sean attempted to pinpoint his roots. Although Teutonic in appearance his slit eyes indicated an additional ethnic mix.

"*Welcome Mr Winters, I'm Jessie, we've been expecting you......*"
He extended his hand in greeting. They shook.

"*So Mr Winters, do you need me to go over anything?*"

"*No I'm all set......*" he said glancing at the V Chamber in bewildered wonder.

"*Good, once you're strapped in, the computer will navigate you accordingly.....it's straight forward....*"

In the moments of silence that followed, the machine started to drone and its door slid open releasing a gush of vapour that instantly dissipated. Sean bit his lips in excitement. He could hear the sound of waking electronic components, which evidently controlled and operated the machine. As he entered, it lit internally, vividly displaying its slick design, and the glittering metal floor, an artefact of highly sophisticated technology. Above him, a hidden device took a beta-wave shot of his brain. An electric-eye....

"*Journey well Sir, you have eight hours of pure pleasure.*"

Sean turned and waved as if actually believing he was about to embark on a global tour.....a journey of a life time....after all it was nothing more than artificial construct, however convincing. The machine itself was partly responsible as it created an aura of its own. Inside, a blank screen encircled him three hundred and sixty degrees. Monitors and machines flickered beneath, bleeping and humming; a whole combination of computerized activity. Dropping into a white chair located in the centre of the chamber, a strap automatically latched itself around him, securing and bolting itself into the floor. Above his head, supported by a thin silver wire, a mask descended, halting as it reached his lap. Then a piercing female voice spoke, as cold ventilated air began pouring in beneath him.

"*Welcome Mr Winters. Please secure the mask onto your face.*"

Rapidly he fitted it, his eyes now staring from beyond the glass view plate of the mask. Again the electric-eye took a wave shot of his brain. It registered, storing the data, displaying it across a luminous screen which ejected from the floor in front of him. An Alpha wave. Eric was now falling into relax mode; this progressive mood change was detected, his brainwaves switching from alpha to theta, higher amplitude lower frequency.

Outside, a technician stood, making final checks, using a reference sheet as his guide. A small component was then inserted into an aperture located to the back of the machine. It fitted perfectly, moulded symmetrically to the precise dimensions of the opening. The V Chamber burst into life with a series of lateral oscillations, lifting into a fixed position above the ground, a metre high. It hung there stationary, defying the laws of gravity. Slowly it began to rotate gathering velocity, until it reached its set speed. Inside, Sean sat calm and focused, unaware and unaffected by its motion. Suddenly the lighting faded, fading into complete darkness, contrary to the tubular screen which now flashed into activity. Displayed across it, was a list of destinations.

"*Please select....*" the voice instructed him.

The chair in which he sat began to revolve, slow but constant. Arm locks folded automatically. Contemplating the list, he thought....'*Africa, I heard so much about its natural beauty....unlike the concrete jungles fashioned by earthly man....Mountains.....Mount Kilimanjaro, three degrees South of the Equator...I'm sure it exists....*' He was flooded with awe and reverence.... "*Africa,*" he yelled, "*Kilimanjaro...*"

Within a fraction of a second, as if space, time and matter had collapsed around him, the raw material of the physical world, he was transported via computerized deception through a dark vacuum. An unyielding darkness replaced everything, sealing him away from reality. Then light, golden sunlight shone around him through thin parting clouds above the shimmering landscape of Tanzania. "*I'm here,*" he said prodding himself, as if for confirmation. "*It's real...*" He could even detect the faint odours that lingered from the rain drenched forests, captivating him as he inhaled each and every scent.

Beneath him, he could feel the soil and undergrowth as he moved his feet in varied directions. Then he saw Kilimanjaro soaring high, penetrating into the atmosphere. In the distance, people and animal roamed alike, faint but definite images of life. His face dripped in sun inflicted perspiration, drops of salty moisture irritating his eyes. '*Amazing,*' he thought, even his body responded chemically to the environment as if he were really there. For the first time he knew what it really felt like to be a part of earthly reality, as if he had been reconnected to the flow of life and time. Away from it was emptiness....darkness....nothing but an indoor world comprised of man-made structures, in order to generate a Terra like environment, but even then nothing like this...this was home....this is where man belonged. Overhead, birds hovered, chirping sounds of communication, darting back and forth, insects buzzing, tiny specks of life, splendour and beauty everywhere, life, life in abundance. Refocusing, he viewed the giant stratovolcano for the last time. With another destination in mind, he said, "*Brazil, the Amazon.....*"

In a flash the scene blurred, swirling away from him in a vortex, with it his sensations and emotions. Again darkness replaced everything, then light. He now stood engulfed by tall trees, sunlight partially filtering through. In the background he captured echoes, echoes that signified life, the dominance of nature. Bending, he saw a coiled gleaming snake, studying its deadly design. It seemed unaware of his existence, its tiny eyes devoid of any spark or awareness. He recalled its lethal venom, a complex mixture of proteins and enzymes but of course it posed no threat, after all it was just a computerized illusion.

He stood calmly, the weight of his feet crunching against the endless green leaves and undergrowth. The air was bug infested, thick and moist, filled with the odour of plants and fetid rot. Across his legs insects crawled, countless kinds, tiny insignificant yet complex organic life. He trudged on through the wild steaming jungle. Around him, shapes moved; vines and leaves dripping with wet slime.

His clothes and face were now saturated in sticky sweat, a result of the scorching heat and stifling humidity. A jaguar then appeared from out of nowhere, its golden reddish brown eyes alive and roaming. The powerful animal prowled in search of prey. Although rigidly conscious of the pseudo environment, Sean froze, his heart constricted, rapidly retrieving its rhythm; metabolic secretions of fear working inside his body. Repressing thalamic impulses he recaptured his composure, reminding himself that it was a plastic reality. But what if it attacked, would it leave inauthentic wounds, scars? Just how real was it all?

Now calm and eager, he gazed upon it, admiring its structure and beauty, staring hard at its tawny yellow fur which was marked with dark spots, clusters of them. *'Its design was too elaborate and perfect to be the product of mere chance,'* he thought. Lunar was governed by an atheistic philosophy, one which he had questioned countless times. Although via powerful telescope he had captured vague images of Earth life, being a part of it was totally different, even though virtual.

Satisfied he moved on feverishly, pushing past a wall of green growth, creepers lodged inside; an elaborate selection buzzing with life. Absorbing as much as the eye could see, he now had the urge for an underwater experience. He reflected, *'the ocean, what must it be like beneath it?'* Summoning courage he yelled, *"The Pacific waters, the Great Barrier Reef!"*

Again, the scene vanished light and life dissolving before him. As darkness parted, he found himself beneath the deep. Instantly, he realised he could breath without the aid of canned air, the one flaw in such a convincing fabricated illusion. The warm blue crystal waters thrived with symbiotic life of all kinds, shapes and sizes, some transparent, glowing, pulsating with brilliant alternating colours; bioluminescence. Beneath him, fixed to the sea floor lay colourful corals; skeletal remains of marine organisms from the class Anthozoa. From the corner of his eye, he saw a giant yet docile manta ray, gliding gracefully towards him, its skin appearing deceivingly smooth.

As it swept past it seemed to enjoy human interaction, responding to Sean's subtle hand signals. Then, he spotted a dolphin, an aquatic mammal, its streamlined fusiform body and distinct beak marking it out from the large fish which encircled it. Again, Sean digested the scene, somewhat philosophically, somewhat passionately. *'Nature, what was the force behind it, what held all things together?'* With a series of forward strokes he moved ahead, awed by the engulfing splendour, even in the deepest depths of Terra, life dwelled. He could now see all kinds of marine life, stone fish, sharks, sea snakes, jellyfish, but one creature in particular amazed him, one he had heard about, in mythological dialogue, an octopus. Via jet propulsion it would move rapidly, uniquely, in contrast to the other species. Sean's face lit with marvel, as he gazed at its tentacles, reflectively. *'What an intricate looking creature, what a complex nervous system it must have.'* He marvelled further as it darted away into the blue...

Having quenched his desire for an underwater experience, he called out, *"Japan......Tokyo."* For some obscure reason he felt the need; a sudden impulse. The sound transmission from his voice catapulted him to yet another destination. Sean now stood on a busy high street, cloud penetrating buildings all around, oriental people rushing in varied directions, young and old alike, beautiful stomach churning aromas assailing his nostrils. Overhead, sky-vehicles hovered, others disappearing beyond the line of the horizon at daring speeds. Stepping from the walkway he crossed the road, impeding mid-afternoon traffic.

Horns beeped, voices rose yelling in foreign tongue. As he reached the other side, he halted, gazing at a neatly clipped tree swaying in the breeze. A magnificent building then caught his attention, one which was able to transform itself into a series of elaborate shapes according to temperature change. To his surprise, an old Japanese man walked over, dressed in a luminous yellow outfit, his face filled with lines of age, his eyes deep-set, blazing with energy, full of expression...... *'so much for an illusion,'* he thought. Although he strolled past him without any interaction, the man appeared excited by his presence. Sean sat resting his heels on the pavement. He moistened his lips, rubbing his chin. *'Where else,'* he pondered, *'where to next?'*

The scenes continued to appear at his command, beautiful landscapes, various destinations, virtual but real, at least real to him, a subjective reality, one which satisfied him fully. Suddenly, there was a flash of intense light which snapped him away from the clutches of the plastic world. Opening his eyes he found himself sitting motionless, staring towards the tubular screen, lit and active, pulsing but blank, mask across his face, streaked with lines of sweat.

"Thank you for journeying with the Virtual Chamber. We look forward to having you aboard again soon......"

Pulling off the mask, the belt automatically released itself, sliding back into the chair for concealment. Again, thoughts began to race through his mind. *How could Lunar and its governing bodies teach atheism? How could they feed people this mathematically illogical philosophy? All things in space and time, every single particle, atom, had to have an origin.....surely? Even the planets which revolved around the life bearing sun were all purposely positioned, spinning at a controlled velocity which allowed life to exist on Earth. Everything throughout the universe is finely balanced, working in symbiosis, equilibrium. If only the people of Lunar had more freedom to journey to Earth on a regular basis they would see its spectacular design and all the life forms that flourish in it, something Lunar was devoid of. Powerful telescopes were not enough to convey the right message......the message that Earth is so very special and that the fabricated worlds elsewhere in the solar system were nothing in comparison to that of this planet. Observation from a distance could never compare. To be a part of earthly existence opened up a whole new way of thinking, about life, the world, the universe, and more importantly our place in it.'*

Heading for the door, it slid open. Calmly, he stepped out and was instantly in contact with a rep, this time a young lady, who beamed at him warmly.

"Mr Winters......how was your trip?"

"Amazing......no words to describe it...... It certainly vindicated the words of the lady who sold me the package, but it's now time for the real thing. I have six days left here......need to sightsee as much as possible...."

"Indeed, New York has many attractions......it even has the first underwater resort, only five miles out across the Atlantic...."

He smiled, recalling his experience, his eyes philosophic and bright. *'As beautiful as it was, the real thing had to be better,'* he thought to himself......

The Man Who Awoke Yesterday

Provoked by a sense of doom, Dirk Allen awoke. Hung-over and with semi-closed eyes he could detect, almost smell, the unfamiliarity of his surroundings. Leaping from the bed in his creased grey suit, he was immediately struck by the crushing fact that his room was no more. Instead he now stood in a luscious apartment, the glazed marble floor dimly reflecting his image. With a trail of clues, the one question remained, where was he? His intuition told him nothing, his anxiety grew as he began to recollect the night past, scrutinizing each and every moment.... *'A few drinks downtown....a cab....then home......What about that blonde chick at the bar? No, I never ended up going back to her place...'* He scratched his chin, head down, eyes on the floor. The whole weird experience was enough to penetrate his alcoholic haze, which was now rapidly fading.

Beyond the door there was motion, a rustling of keys commingling with the vocal chimes of happiness. As the door swung open a woman walked in, her svelte frame clothed in a pink dress, exposing most of her shapely thighs. Flinging off her high heels, she paused and shot him a glance.....

"*Good day Dirk,*" she said with her deep southern accent, her eyes bright blue, full of confidence and self satisfaction.

"*You're not bad looking at all......just as I specified.*"

A series of puzzled expressions flashed across his face. With a big teeth-exposing grin, she turned strolling barefoot into the adjoining kitchenette, her damp feet leaving faint imprints across the marble floor. Incensed by the chain of wacky events, he rushed over shaking his head.

"*Look here lady, what's this all about......?*"

He began to twist and turn, absorbing the surroundings.....

"*Who are you anyway......how did I get here?*"

"*Dirk sweetheart,*" she replied. "*Now that you are here with me......nothing else in this universe should matter......*"

He frowned with a piercing silent stare. His eyes did not waver from her.

"*Listen lady, I haven't time for games...I'm not following your drift...*"

"*It's simple.*" She brushed back her blond locks. "*You are, because I say......*"

For a brief moment he considered her words, but could make nothing of them.

"*Let's start again......*" He shook his head.

"*Dirk.....you're just not understanding me are you?*

She eyed him intently, resting a hand on her hip.

"*Let's put it like this......you are a construct of my mind....today is your time to be a part of my world......a part of my existence....*"

"*Sure,*" he muttered acidly, "*I get it....you're the local fruitcake, I just happened to run into......right?...Sorry mam, it's time for me to rejoin the real world!!!*"

"*Dirk......!*"

Turning to go, he froze, his legs stiffening into immobility, as if the woman's voice held some kind of magnetic property. Although he felt in control, he didn't move.

"*Sweetheart, you're not the first guy to react like this, and certainly not the last......*"

Motionless, he listened, backing down lamely, his face pale and drawn.

"*Out there you're nothing without me...whether you like it or not......you can't just pick up and leave...*"

"*So what are you suggesting then?*"

"*Just that......*"

Her eyes rolled amorously, her long dark lashes fluttering. Enraged by her dismissive care-free attitude, he raised his hand pointing at her, breaking free from his hypnotic daze.....

"*That does it.....I'm out of here....*"

Hurrying to the door, he left, descending down a flight of dusty stairs towards the exit below. On a busy Chicago sidewalk, Dirk moved sluggishly towards home mixing in with the flow of people and noise, hands deep inside his trouser pockets, shoulders sagging with fatigue. '*That half-crazed chick, what was that all about? She was cute though. Must have been really out of it.....*' Suddenly he thought of home.... But where was it? Betrayed by his memory, he paused mystified, his features contorting as he pondered deeper, thinking at high speed. '*That's it, how could I forget? Ellisville, Ellisville's home......*'

At the smog filled train station, Dirk walked over to the ticket office, dollars in hand.

"*Where to, Buddy....?*" Jackson, the ticket clerk asked, puffing away at a cigar, his thinning hair hanging over his face and ears.

"*Ellisville please......*"

"*Where...?*"

"*Ellisville......*"

"*Never heard of it...*"

"*What......?*"

"*You heard......*" he said, regarding him sharply.

"*Wait a minute......are you telling me......?*"

"*Yes, that's right......now if you wouldn't mind, I have a line of people behind you waiting to buy tickets...*"

Jackson's voice was filled with frustration as he leaned on the counter, peering closely into his face. Dirk glanced over his shoulder at the long line of people. Men and women stood there alike, grumbling and rolling their eyes impatiently. Turning back to the ticket clerk, he said, "*Look Mr, I've lived there most my life...there must be some kind of mistake.*"

Jackson's mouth opened and closed, but no sound came. Then he pointed at the half dangling chart board with a finger.

"*Look, a list of all the stops, but no Ellisville....satisfied?*"

Dirk studied it anxiously, but it wasn't there. Not a trace of it, as if it had been wiped out of existence. From behind, he felt a cold hand tug at him.

"*Hey, what's going on?*" a middle-aged suited man complained, adjusting his glasses. "*I've got to be at work in the next ten minutes.*"

He tapped his wrist at an imaginary watch. Clutching onto him with trembling hands Dirk spoke, his voice choking with emotion, "*Sir perhaps you can help....?*"

The man eyed him up and down, switching his focus towards Jackson and back.

"*Ellisville......you've heard of Ellisville....right?*" Dirk's voice sank with desperate pleading hope.

"*Never heard of it......*"

"*But.....but how can that be...?*"

The stabbing reality was too much to take in as it reached his conscious mind. Brutal, overt fear had taken over, distorting his features and stance, inner forces conspiring, working, pulling him emotionally

Anthony Fucilla

apart. In an instant, Dirk released his grip on the man and darted away, almost losing his footing, the line of people turning and grumbling in bewildered annoyance.

Under dim lights, in a downtown bar, Dirk swept back his third shot of bourbon, straining it down, his head moving to the melodic notes uttered from the jukebox in the corner. The alcohol had now taken effect as it rose up inside him, mildly suppressing his natural emotions and reactions. Then, sliding a quarter into a pay phone beside the bar, he dialled amidst a maze of empty beer bottles.

"*Hello,*" a voice murmured groggily.

"*Rita, please listen to me.....just give me a second...*"

"*Listen Mr, can you stop calling, this is the third time today....I don't know you.....good day!*"

The phone slammed down; Dirk's heart constricted, flooding his body with a cold tingling sensation, the dim lights concealing his fright filled features.

"*Damn,*" he cried, banging his fist against the counter......

His mind suddenly went blank, as if he had lost his identity, and had become an inanimate object. His whole world was now in jeopardy. He recalled little, but even more bizarre yet, no-one seemed to remember him or his little home town of Ellisville. Who was he? What were these memories and past recollections he had? How could he trust them? That woman, who was she? What was she? Could it be he was a creation of someone's will, stepping through a series of windows into different times...dimensions, a metaphysical multiplexity of realities?

Across from him, in silence, the bar tender indicated another shot, making a drinking motion with his hand. In reply Dirk shook his head. Then from behind him, someone squeezed his arm. He turned, and there before him stood the unknown woman, dolled up, oozing with confidence and panache, beaming at him warmly.

"*Hi gorgeous......*"

Dirk swallowed hard, and drew breath, body tense.

"*Who are you? What do you want from me?*"

She smiled, teeth sparkling white in the half light. With her cold bony hand she began toying with the buttons of his shirt. With slow twisting facial motions, she unfastened one.

"*You hun......you wouldn't be here otherwise....*"

She leaned over to kiss him, lips pouting. Raising his hand he pushed her away.

"*Stop talking in riddles*," Dirk protested, his voice faltering, his breath reeking with alcohol.

"*Dirk love, you must understand one thing...*"

She lit a cigarette, the tip glowing red as she took a steady puff, directing it into his face.

"*All that you are is because of me......and this is why you partially exist in this world of mine......*"

Choking, he waved his hand into the quickly fading smoke, his eyes semi-closed and red rimmed.

"*Partially...? You could have fooled me.*" He touched his face with both hands, as if examining......a sarcastic gesture to reinstate his existence...

"*Dirk, you are really hard headed.*" She puffed again, marking the cigarette with her red lipstick.

"*Don't you get it yet? Dirk Allen never existed, at least not here......maybe in another universe, another time, you were a part of someone else's world, someone else's reality....but here you are mine......solely mine...*"

There was a moment of silence, as if there was a hidden twisted truth in what she was saying. An inconceivable terrifying truth......

"*I don't get it!*"

"*Don't try, you never will......just enjoy your time for what it lasts....and at this rate not very long...*"

"*What's that supposed to mean?*"

"*Just as I willed you into existence,*" she lowered her gaze, smirking, a cold secret smirk, "*I can quite easily will you out...Remember you're only a construct of my mind......*"

His eyes grew wide and envenomed.

"*Do you really think I believe this garbage?*" He yelled.

His voice increased in volume and confidence. Then, he reflected. The one undeniable problem which lingered deep inside him, was the fact she was the only thing that made him feel alive and real, nullifying that absurd inexplicable void within. It gave him hope, a sense of certainty, a sense of being, yet he refused to accept the necessity of her presence.

"*What about......?*"

"*Dirk,*" she said sharply, halting him midway through his sentence....
"*Don't talk about memories, they are yours....perhaps from another time and place......but here they mean nothing....*"

"*Hey, how did you know what I was going to say?*"

"*I've heard it a million times over.....you're not the first...and you won't be the last...*"

Stubbing out her cigarette against the counter, she dropped it to the floor grinding it down with her heel.

"*Come......lets go take a ride......*"

Pulling him by his crumpled grey jacket, she led him outside into the parking lot. There was a chill wind, sharp and penetrating, a line of trees swaying, bending furiously. The cold instantly roused him. Shakily, he crossed his arms pressing them against his chest. Above, the clouds dispersed, almost vanishing, leaving the skyline bare, unveiling the dim night spheres in the slowly growing gloom.

"*Where are you taking me?*"

"*Dirk, you know something......you ask too many questions...*"

Walking over to a bright silver Mustang, she stepped in opening the passenger door.

"*Hop in......*" she said coaxingly, starting the motor, revving the engine.

He stood at the door awkwardly, uncertain whether to enter, tempted purely by curiosity. The wind began nudging and biting into him, almost forcing him into the car, as if the elements had conspired to lure him into the clutches of the unknown woman.

"*Come on sweetheart, this in our night, the first of many....*"

Grim faced he entered, gazing at her with opposing emotions. Turning, he looked ahead through the moisture stained windscreen, feeling acutely helpless. What was next?

Down a wide city road, they moved swiftly, odometer racing cars and motorbikes zooming past, tiny dark specks rushing through the evening twilight.

"*Can you please tell me where we are going...?*"

"*You know something? Of all the guys, you're the one who's really given me a hard time......time is all you have......so enjoy it......*"

The glow and sparkle in her eyes began to diminish to a more serious and cynical look, almost cadaverous, as if all life had melted away within her. For a time there was silence, neither of them spoke. Tall grey street lights suddenly activated, illuminating the city. Darkness had now descended; pitch black. Ahead, he could see neon lights, green, red and blue, music pumping, vibrating and echoing, chaos everywhere. Clubs and bars filled the streets, row after row of night activity, youngsters swarming around chatting, mumbling meaningless sounds.

Pulling over, she yanked the brakes, killing the drive in an instant; a sickening jolt. Vigour for life had now returned to her.

"*Come, let's party......*"

A parking attendant walked up immediately from beyond the restless crowds, tipping his cap.

"*Sorry mam....this is a tow-away zone....*"

"*But I can park here, right...?*"

"*Right, take as long as you like....have a great night mam.*"

"*What,*" Dirk gasped, astonished at the attendant's reaction.

Pushing through a long line, she walked up to the entrance of a club, Dirk following desperately behind, sweat trickling down his neck and into his collar. Without a word, two burly bouncers parted, revealing the elegant entrance. A gold coloured carpet lay there; elaborate patterns woven into it.

"*Have a wonderful night, mam......*" they muttered timidly, half bowing.

Dirk followed, puffing and red faced. Grabbing his arm, she steered him through the plush doors, towards the rhythmic rumble of sound and motion. In the middle of a small brown table an artificial candle burned. Facing each other, they sat in silence, throwing sporadic glances around the dance floor.

"*Tell me Dirk, do you like dancing? I love the way people express their emotions....feelings through different sounds......*" She rocked her head to the rackety beats.

"*No,*" he snapped with a sudden flicker of aversion, his voice rising above the blaring music which sent faint vibrations across the table.

"*Where would you like to live? I've always fancied Denver.*" For a brief moment she closed her eyes dreamily, crossing her legs..."*Those beautiful mountains, all that fresh air.....wooden cabin....oak fireplace.*"

"*Anywhere away from you would be ideal.....*"

"*Oh dear,*" she gasped. "*What's wrong now?*"

"You....this...all this...." He stood up nervously, waving his arms in the air, sitting moments later. *"I can't believe I'm actually here listening to you..."*

His whole approach had now reversed. The cooperative attitude that had brought him thus far had somehow reverted, acting like a catalyst, bringing back those negative emotions in him. He was caught in a cycle of negativity. Yet in the back of his mind, unanswered questions roamed plucking at him every now and then....Ellisville.....his vague memories of it....this lady, his gut feelings. Where would he go from here? *'Away from her,'* he thought, *'away from her would be a start.....'*

"Dirk, I'm beginning to realise we are not meant for each other......"

"No kidding lady...."

"I don't think you understand......without me you cease to be......this is my world......an entire world revolving around me...."

"Well that's kinda strange, because you and I ain't going anywhere......"

A waiter walked over, his eyes bright in the candle light.

"Drinks...?"

She shook her head signalling no, then indicated five minutes with her bony hand.

"Tell me......what makes you believe that this world is yours anyway?"

"That's just how it is, that's just how it has always been. You are a part of it because I willed you into being......The only real living thing in this world is me......all that you see is partially real..."

"So I don't exist.....in fact, no one does but you right?"

"Kind of....."

"So if this is your world, and you can have anything you want....why is it from the very moment we met, I've been trying to avoid you?"

"True love has to come naturally, it can't be forced..." She smiled; a cold humourless smile.

"This has gone far enough.....Theoretically speaking, am I to believe I'm some lingering, partial existent entity...surrounded by an illusionary world of your creation?"

"Theoretically......" she replied, her voice tinged with patronizing overtones.

"Right, that's it.....no more games......it ends here...."

Dirk leapt up and darted towards the exit, barging past a crowd of drunkards, the woman following closely behind. Out in the cold night, the city streets were almost bare.

"*Dirk....do you realise what this means? I don't think you do.*"

He halted, and turned.

"*Yes....yes in fact I do....you and me finish here....read my lips.*" He pointed at his mouth. "*Goodbye......Oh, just one thing before I go...purely out of curiosity, what is your name......?*"

"*What does it matter now......you and I ain't meant to be...right Dirk?*"

"*Right....*" He shook his head; his cheeks flushed red with indignation. "*I can't believe I've played along with this......perhaps we'll meet in another time, another dimension......*"

He walked off hunched over, entering a dark bare section of the city. Nothing moved. Detecting faint clattering footsteps he turned spotting her in the moonlight, the wind whistling around him.

"*You still ain't getting it are you? I'm out of here...*"

In the blink of an eye, Dirk puffed out of existence. All that remained where he stood was a smoky haze which quickly faded, dissipating into the void. Gazing at the empty space he had occupied, she turned and began strolling back to the car, a circle of light engulfing her. No matter how long she waited, she was bound to get it right sometime......the right one had to come sooner or later......

Slit in the Sky

"Professor Western, are you certain that all earth life originated from aliens......?"

The cam-crew focused in, lights from the studio shining towards him. He smiled eyes fixed and arrogant, beaming with reflected glory.

"Yes...yes indeed I am...."

He adjusted his necktie, his chest swelling with pride.

"In recent years it was only a plausible theory, a hypothesis to be exact, but now, as we speak, it's absolute fact."

The audience sat in stunned silence, the host referring to his digital-note-screen.

"But how Mr Western, how can you be certain....what tangible evidence do you have....?"

Slowly the images began to fade, fading away from him, and now in a daze of timeless half sleep he awoke, the ceiling jet vent spraying him with a morning dose of bacterial repellent. Instantly he registered with reality, detecting movement, as the auto-coffee maker wheeled itself towards the bed, halting in the half shadow of the room. Sipping a cup languidly he washed, changed, and was now ready for his appointment with the Atlantic City Times. He had five minutes. Darting down the stairs into his study, he stepped into his newly invented Trans-propeller, a tall narrow metallic unit, its interior gleaming wickedly with lights, knobs and switches of all kinds.

"Eric darling," the nagging voice of his wife rasped. *"What time will you be back..?"*

"As soon as I'm done....."

"Thank goodness you've got a unit installed back at the office. It was taking you hours to get back home through the busy commercial lanes, that endless tide of traffic....."

She walked into the study stirring a cup of nutra-vite mineral drink, its foul odour mixing in with the scent of his cologne.

"Tina, I wish you'd stop drinking that....the only way you'll ever lose weight is if you stop eating," he barked, rolling his eyes away from her, back to the monitor, his face ablaze with technological know how.

Dismissively, stubbornly she replied.... *"How long will it be before the T-propeller is sold commercially?"*

"*That's for the government to decide.....it won't be easy to stop all air-cruisers and surface vehicles....too many credits involved...highly political.*" He shook his head in annoyance. Then, turning a dial with careful deliberation he was gone in a flash, the unit vibrating faintly, glowing dimly red.

Eric Western reappeared at his office, beside a T-propeller, a slightly modified version, in contrast to the one back home. It was bigger, more spacious and elaborate. Adjusting his tie he sat at his desk, peering out of the window, contemplating the scene. Air-cruisers were landing in swarms, roads choked with traffic and people dashing to work. Calmly he lit a cigar, leaning back. It flared, burning red hot, infesting the room with smoke. He sucked in expertly, puffing out, pride and achievement etched into his features. He had started the day exactly right, fresh and unfazed as always. There was a knock at the door, then another; a frightened repetitive tap.

"*Come in Wendy,*" he snapped, recognising the distinctive knock. The cute faced receptionist turned the handle, popping her head around the door, blushing sweetly.

"*Professor.....Mr Coin from the ACT Newspaper is here to see you...*"

"*Great! Bring him through......*"

He stubbed out his cigar in the hydro-tray, sitting upright, professional. Suddenly, a rugged looking man stumbled in, briefcase in one hand, hanky in the other. He was dressed in a creased blue suit, his shirt collar loose and open, a black tie hanging from it.

"*James Coin ......ACT....*"

They shook. A tight firm shake......

"*Professor Western.....delighted to meet you...*"

The name thundered in his ears with ripples of awe.

"*I can't believe it......I'm standing in front of history...is it really you......the greatest pioneer since Walter Stevenson?*"

Eric nodded with a smile.....

"*Please Mr Coin, take a seat.*"

He indicated the chair on the opposite side of the desk.

"*Tell me....just curious......Were you always fascinated with machines....as a kid I mean...?*"

"Yes I was. My father once told me that man is a machine maker, constructing greater and more complex working elements....from that day on, I developed an interest...."

"Okay.....back to business. As you know I'm here about your invention....the....." He paused......

*"T-propeller,"....*Eric said in a low modulated voice, pointing towards it. James' eyes followed his hand, his face slightly flushed with relief.

"That's it......keep forgetting the name," he replied in stunned admiration..... *"Wow, it looks even more complex than the photos portray....years of designing, planning, and careful calculation......"*

He turned, now facing Eric.

"You've made history Professor......Citizens all over the US and overseas have been raving about it....Now tell me, give me a brief run down on how it operates......its benefits..."

He opened his briefcase, pulling out his digi.

"With all due respect, the mathematical formula is unique and strictly confidential....there are things I would rather keep private.....even then the explanation would be far too mind boggling for you to grasp......with regard to its benefits...well that's self evident......is it not?"

*"In your own words please"....*James said as he activated the registering vocalizer.

Eric got up, pacing around the room in thought, hands behind his back.

"The T-propeller was designed to catapult a person or object to a set destination anywhere in the globe, to the specific location of your choice by the use of an intricate co-ordinate mechanism.....and hopefully soon, other parts of our solar system and galaxy.....planets that are well known holiday destinations, like Mars, with no time lapse, consequently revolutionizing space travel and indeed all forms of travel as we know it..."

"Mars....That's great Professor, I have relatives there.....The sooner the better...I hate the journey....but you mention the word hopefully......Why?"

"At present I have no proof that it can work outside of this planet......it still needs to be tested....but I am certain it will.... To summarize, there will be no need of air-cruisers or surface vehicles, here on Earth.....it will be a thing of the past...."

James checked the digi as the words uttered danced across the screen, the vocalizer working efficiently, rapidly.

"*Please continue....*"

"*It's almost a 70 mile trek from home to work...it took me less than a second...no headaches....no sky or road traffic, no stress or speeding tickets......and no excuses from late employees....once commercially on the market....of course!*"

James smiled in amusement...."*You were last quoted saying, only a few weeks back, that the device operates by bridging distances, non-spacially.....through,*" he cut off recalling.... "*...through another dimension, correct?*"

"*I've already made it clear once, Mr Coin....*" He raised his hand to affirm the point. "*I will not disclose any more information on technical methods.....or go into the physics of it for that matter......*"

"*Fine......but please...hear me out...*"

Eric halted, peering down at him.

"*During that brief second of launch where do you go? You must go somewhere! When on the market, buyers will demand to know....and you as manufacturer will be forced to answer... a factual answer, please Professor...*"

"*Okay....fine,*" Eric said reluctantly, now sitting, leaning back against his flexible chair, legs crossed.

"*Let's just say you are catapulted into another dimension...out of this continuum....*"

The digi registered with a series of clicks.

"*How many units have you built to date?*"

"*Ten. Eight are kept back at the workshop....the other two I use....one here, one at home......*"

"*Any initial defects....?*"

"*Would I be looking to put it on the market? No....of course not,*" he bristled indignantly. "*My two technicians and I went through thousands of vigorous tests....no failures.....no defects......we had formulated a list of dates for periodic inspection.*"

"*How long do you estimate it will be before it is sold to the general public....?*"

"*Can't answer that right now, the political implications are vast, invention could destabilise the planet...society. Businesses will collapse worldwide....ones like EPO and Jefferson Engineering, companies that are responsible for constructing surface vehicles and air-cruisers will all go bust......and many others will inevitably follow. It's simply not as easy as you think. It's a major leap from what we are used to, a total transition......there has to be time for adjustment, time for the major change....the travel and transport industry will totally die because of my invention. Only I, as creator, designer and manufacturer of the T-propeller can legally use one at present....and enjoy all its benefits....but due to my altruistic tendencies, I hope that will soon change."*

He wiped perspiration from his forehead with his hand.

"Any drawbacks with the unit......?"

"One......An obvious one......"

"Which is?" James asked, somewhat alarmed by his reply...

"In order to travel back to the point of launch in the same manner....wherever it may be, you would need another unit at your destination....Like me for example, one unit here, one at home...."

"So what you're saying is...if I travelled to Mars with the T-propeller, I would need another unit there in order to get back the same way I got there...."

"Exactly, but as I said, that's obvious....which brings me to my next point...."

The phone-com rattled across the desk, breaking the flow of the discussion. Turning a dial he terminated the call.

"As I was saying...my next point is I have a serious problem..."

"Excuse me...what problem? I've lost you...."

An interval of silence passed....

"My friend, I'm about to reveal something to you....something I haven't shared with anyone..."

"Please continue Professor......"

"I'm planning to attempt a journey beyond our galaxy....beyond what we know, using the T-propeller......"

"But you said it still needs to be tested....and that's in relation to our solar system....our galaxy. But why......"

Eric interjected.

"James.....if I can prove it works in our solar system and indeed galaxy.....there's no reason to believe it won't work outside of it....my only problem, a serious problem, would be getting back. I'm targeting the galaxy Andromeda. I've been planning it, studying it, even dreaming of it...."

"But why journey to other parts of the universe where nothing exists.....or at least there is no certainty of any life....or means of transportation back? Never mind the T-propeller......"

With a swift motion of his hand, he deactivated the digi.

"My friend...my mission is solely one, to prove that alien life exists. I have a theory that life on Earth was created by extraterrestrials......To prove this to myself, and the

world, depending on whether or not I could get back of course, would mean having to go there......"

"*Ok.....but where exactly is Andromeda?*" James asked.

"*Nearby......relatively speaking of course......2.2 million light years away......a place beyond, a leap into the unknown. Naturally I would have to target one specific planet within the galaxy, making all the correct calculations. It's a journey I'm compelled to take, whatever the consequences, life or death......"*

"*But......but what are the odds of finding aliens there? I mean it's such a gamble, and after all, none have been seen in our galaxy......what makes you believe you'll find them elsewhere?*

What concrete evidence do you have......?"

"*None.....but I do have an old book, written by a very famous Astrophysicist, Henry Wicks, claiming to have been visited by aliens from the galaxy Andromeda.....He was told no other race of aliens existed, other than theirs, and that their race inhabited every planet within their galaxy, and that they all originated from the planet Ius...This makes my job a lot easier....all I need do is choose one planet.*"

"*So in short, you are prepared to journey into the depths of the universe to prove that nothing else is responsible for creating life on Earth, other than these aliens mentioned in an old book......even at the cost of your life, with no tangible evidence of their existence other than a theory, and the words of a man?*"

"*Correct....In essence, I'm a modern day Christopher Columbus.....He crossed the vast expanse of the Atlantic with a dream....I'll journey into the emptiness of space with another.....only that mine is a far bigger challenge to say the least......"*

"*Well...*" James said placing his digi into his briefcase. "*I guess that wraps things up.....*" He got up. "*Thank you for your time.*"

He reached out a moist palm and they shook; a delighted friendly shake.

"*I'll have the credits sent straight through to your account. We'll be in touch......and good luck...*"

Startled, James walked out, closing the door behind. For a moment Eric wondered why he cut off so quickly, so abruptly. Had something he said triggered off his prompt exit, or was it just him....his usual bout of crazed paranoia. Consulting his table clock he decided, that was that. Raising the phone-com, he pressed a button and was put through with visual transmission. He could now see his wife in the bathroom humming, singing and splashing, bare and pink under a steaming hot shower.

"*Hi honey*," she cried out piercingly in an attempt to speak over the sound of the running water. "*Are you coming home?*"

Across the screen the images soon became cloudy, as the quickly forming moisture partially masked the view.

"*Yes....be there in approximately three minutes....*"

"*Okay, I'll go prepare you a snack...your favourite selection of sandwiches...*"

"*Great.*"

Stepping out of the shower, she lifted a blue towel from the floor with the aid of her toe. Wrapping the warm fabric around her she smiled and waved. As he disconnected, the scenes vanished. Arranging the phone-com into its usual position, he yelled, "*Wendy.*" There was movement, heels tapping against the floor. The door opened.

"*Yes.*"

"*I'm off. Take all messages for me, or rather, re-circulate them to my home number, if urgent. See you in the morning.*"

"*Okay Professor.....*"

Rising from his chair he walked over and entered the T-propeller through the revolving doors. Above his head, lights and bulbs glowed, periodically, sequentially. Gazing at the control board, his fingers flew into activity, and in a flash he was gone, faster than light.

Eric Western reappeared in what looked like a hazy grey tubular tunnel. Immediately, without panicking he realised he had somehow been caught between his world and the other, trapped in a bubble between reality and the other dimension as he had explained it. The tunnel stretched like a pipe with no visible end. There was no sound or motion, other than the audible beating of his heart. The whole experience had a dreamlike, sluggish quality to it.

With measured steps he began to walk. The ground beneath him was real, substantial, even his footsteps faintly echoed. He was engulfed in awe, nullifying all his natural emotions and biological instincts......fear, desperation, worry......doom. His features were twisting in a strange excitement, trance-like in overwhelming disbelief. As he reached the end, there was no cut off point as such, no barrier or wall, just a luminous glaze, and something inside it moved. Approaching it face on, he bent slowly. Amazingly his office came into view.

It was presented to him as if watching it from a small circular vision-screen, yet the image was indistinct, blurry, milky, wavering, and from it no sound came. He could see his mahogany desk and chair, his library of books, atlas globe and fishing rods, even his portrait hanging on the wall. Then Wendy walked in, documents in hand, dim and distorted almost lost in the blurry haze. Reaching out towards the thin shimmer of existence, his hand was immediately repelled, jolting back as if hit by a bolt of electricity. There was no lingering pain, just a mild tingle.

Frightened, he instinctively stood, and began racing towards the other end as fast as he could, but his legs soon betrayed him. He halted regaining breath and continued on, walking at a slow pace until he reached the far end. There he could see his house, his wife standing at the kitchen table preparing sandwiches and drinking her usual fix of coffee, even the rays of sunlight penetrating through the half pulled blinds. Again it was blurry, milky.....seemingly a step away, but in reality further than conceivably possible. Desperation and fear overwhelmed him. '*Tina......!*' he cried, his voice echoing and booming, but it was futile. He could now see his wife wandering away from the shimmer, disappearing into the vague depths of the other world.

Then suddenly, above his head, as if space, the universe itself had opened up before him, there was darkness. This darkness extended down the length of the tunnel as far as the eye could see. He stood in terrified immobility. In a flash the solar system appeared before him.....Neptune, Saturn, Jupiter, indeed all the planets revolving around the sun, like an atomic structure. The images changed. Now he could see the other worlds......galaxies, Andromeda, a spectrum of colours and varying patterns, hostile moisture-stripped planets, dull rotating spheres naked and barren, toxic atmospheres, dark cold crumpled rock....layer after layer.

The expanding universe was now displayed in its totality, how and why he didn't know, but somehow in this dimension the images continued to roll....but no signs of alien life. '*Where were they?*' he wondered, his theory beginning to collapse within him. Perhaps something else was responsible for creating man....life on

Earth....something far greater than he could imagine...something beyond time and space and far more superior to imaginary aliens. The words of Astrophysicist Henry Wicks had proven to be lies......his book was nothing but fabrication. Eric's distorted philosophy now faded into nothingness as other galaxies flashed before him, comets speeding through the universe, some consumed and swallowed into unknown forbidden planets. Still he looked on in fascination....but no signs of life anywhere.

Suddenly, he was drawn towards the shimmering scene of his existence by an invisible energy field. In a flash and with a faint pop, as if the imaginary bubble of his dwelling had burst, he found himself inside his study at home, beside the T-propeller.

Sweating profusely, he looked up, gripping onto reality, his reality as he knew it. Then to his overwhelming relief, he heard his wife's voice. He was now certain he had escaped the clutches of the other dimension.

"Honey....you took your time."

He rubbed his eyes orienting himself, pale and exhausted.....stripped of his dignity.

"Are you okay?"

"Yes I'm fine," he mumbled, in a daze.

"By the way, Brett Anderson just called, he needed to speak to you urgently....your invention may get on the market sooner than expected......"

"Really," he said, collapsing into his gold leather chair......his lip curled. He motioned for the chair-manipulator to bring him a shot of brandy. He was in desperate need.

"I can't wait. Soon the entire planet will benefit from your marvellous invention. Hundreds of years from now you'll be remembered as one of the world's greatest pioneers.....Eric hun, they don't know what's in store for them...."

He turned, gazed at it nervously, eyes round and wide......

"Yes indeed......they certainly don't......"

The Appointment

"*Hear me out....*" Earth Leader Vic Matuzak croaked, pointing, his aging face alight with strict command. "*As the appointed Ambassador of this planet the responsibility lies solely with you....*" He raised his brow, his eyes peering intently, almost predatory.

"*I hope I've made myself perfectly clear? Either they comply or else.......!*"

"*Yes Sir....*"

"*Remember no sting of conscience...no sentiment...*"

Ludovic stood, saluted and turned almost rhythmically in military fashion, walking towards the door....

At the government headquarters Ludovic Martel sat at his oak desk, document in hand, his ashtray filled with cigarette-butts, the office redolent with its lingering stench. A lot was on his mind. In the walls hidden machinery whirred, discharging periodic wafts of ice cold air into the room. Suddenly, the intercom buzzed into life......

"*Sir......Jake De Quent is here....*"

"*Okay Roger, escort him up,*" he grumbled with an elaborated casualness, continuing about his day.

A few minutes later Jake walked in, composed as always.

"*Hi Lud.....how was the meeting?*"

"*Okay I guess...just the same message......We're scheduled to leave tomorrow.....*"

"*Yes I was told......*"

"*What about you Jake, how's the research going?*"

Sitting he replied......

"*Good....real good...I've been working furiously at the Cosmic Centre......looking over this planet Orious....Still find it hard to believe that it took us so long to discover it.....we had all the systems mapped out....every planet.....*"

"*Well, it is located in another region of our galaxy. Who knows what lies out there.....the endless universe, a dark vacuum of limitless dimensions......*" Ludovic cut off, gazing at him wearily with glazed eyes....

"*I guess so......sixty thousand light years away....Hopefully we won't run into any meteor swarms before we reach the wormhole......*"

From his jacket, he pulled out a document, unrolling it......

"*Here,*" he chimed eagerly, lips pressed together. "*All the essential information in regards to Orious.....It's all there, climate, temperature, its fixed periodic seasons, soil type, mineral deposits, air density, fauna and flora....very similar to here......almost uncanny....an oxygen nitrogen mix atmosphere......"*

Ludovic stretched it out across the desk, scanning through, using a finger for guidance...his lips moving silently.

"It's the only known planet Lud....the only one in this entire galaxy which stands on its own.....away from our rule."

Jake's eyes grew wide with anticipation as he contemplated his own words.....

"And even after two long meetings with their representatives here on Earth, they still remain adamant, stubborn....they simply refuse to be a part of the galactic circle..."

"For the moment......" Ludovic replied sharply. *"You see Jake, our visit there will change things......"*

"I doubt it. They are locked into their own system...an ancient religious system of some type, I believe.....besides....they've known about us for years...According to their leader, Earth has been a planet they have taken great interest in, analysing it from their com-modules, checking us out, studying it rigorously. In all that time they have never once wanted to contact us....or any of our colonies. That in itself tells the story...."

"You'll be surprised how things can change with the right application....."

"Lud, between you and me I'm not too sure about this one. They will never conform to the galactic culture or law....It's as if they purposely want to maintain a religious archaic like existence, even though it appears to keep up with our technocratic levels....at least from what we know....They certainly appear to have made similar progressive advancements on their own......who knows? Perhaps they have other things that we don't know of...greater things, greater inventions.... "

"Regardless Jake, the purpose of this trip is to send them a message....a final ultimatum...either they sign...."

His face became hard and cynical. He clenched his fist...his eyes held no emotion.

"Or...?"

"Or, we blow them out of existence......"

The immense ship entered the planet's atmosphere...swooping towards a giant space-port, in a glowing blur of energy. Dials and meters swung into activity, registering, humming. Descent lights flickered. Across the gleaming control board, the co-pilot spun a dial releasing a series of signals, which the base monitor below recorded.

"I've received clearance," the co confirmed to the head pilot.

Rapidly, with precision, they descended, the landscape of the planet now coming into view. As the ship landed, a tide of energy shook the ground. Acceleration dials fell to zero. At last they had arrived after a four day journey. Technicians suddenly appeared, rushing out from small surveillance-huts, busy little dots dressed in grey, circling around the ship, inspecting for metal fatigue and stress fractures; structural damage. Ship monitoring surface-vehicles lurched from side to side, a bustle of efficient motion.

Both Ludovic and Jake walked down the ramp with eager strides, gazing around arrogantly. A surge of adrenaline raced through them. Overhead, the sky was dull and cloudy, the air humid and hot. Barren fields surrounded the space-port, burned clean of any vegetation, beyond it an undulating expanse of green, a verdant countryside which stretched towards a metropolis, a tiny flickering dot in the distance.

"*Do you realise Jake, we are finally here......we've made history.....but it's imperative we remain focused on the task.....*"

A long blue vehicle suddenly pulled up, creeping to a halt. An elegantly dressed man stepped out from the driver's seat and calmly walked over, his heels clattering against the ground. He was tall and slim, his blue eyes warm.

"*Clarence Marvin, Cultural Attaché...and for today your driver as well....*" He half bowed and smiled his face aglow with sincerity......

"*Ludovic Martel, Terra Ambassador.*" He shook his hand awkwardly with mixed emotions, folder under his arm. "*This is Professor Jake De Quent, Chief Scientist for the government.*"

"*How nice to meet you both.....please let's make our way, our leader is anticipating your arrival....we have exactly one hour before the meeting at the palace. You'll both find the back seats very comfortable...*"

They were on a hot steaming highway, blending in with the endless tide of surface-vehicles. Ludovic sat in silence gazing through the window at the green countryside. In the distance a winged creature hovered, skimming the surface of the planet. The clouds had now subsided. The sun shone and the sky sparkled into being, restoring light and colour to the land, trees and hills, the endless valleys. Above, jets hummed, circling the sky, commuters returning from work, slender metallic crafts of countless kinds.

"You've got some neat looking jets here, Mr Marvin...."

"Oh yes Mr Martel, indeed we do.....They are the latest and very special.....free from the force of gravity...."

"What....! You mean to say you have anti-gravity technology...?"

"Yes, newly discovered...an amazing technological invention. When our representatives journeyed to Earth for those two recent meetings, they used an anti-gravity ship....."

Ludovic and Jake gazed at each other in total astonishment....

"Did you hear that Jake? Incredible! You were right......" Ludovic whispered in his ear.....*"Indeed they do have other things...things that we can benefit from, once we take over....."*

Silence resumed......

"By the way, gentlemen, just for your information, we are about to enter the robot quarters of the city..."

"Robot quarters....? What kind of government would implement such a law, segregating robots from humans?" Ludovic muttered to himself nudging Jake, who seemed equally perturbed.

"Mr Marvin, have you always had this city set up this way...humans one part of the city, robots the other....?"

"Yes of course, Mr Martel.....as liberal as we are, we've always understood that man and machine must live separately...machines are there for the sole purpose to serve man......nothing more.....of course they are treated with respect, but each to their own.....Most take on economic and industrial functions......"

Jake interrupted......*"You see, down on Earth....and throughout the galaxy, robots live with humans functioning in unanimity....."*

"I can believe it....but not here......"

The surface-vehicle took a sharp turn, *'Exit Wallisberg.'* Passing through a long winding tunnel they entered a huge city, a cacophony of endless sounds. Chaos filled the air. Robots were scattered everywhere, bright hulls of metal standing in groups, conversing, streaming in and out of buildings, speeding on glider bikes, each and everyone engaged in some kind of activity. Further on, a conglomeration of towering structures soared into the atmosphere, endless spires rising up like needles, diffusing a golden glow, emanating from the specialised alloys.

"Quite an advanced looking city Mr Marvin..." Ludovic said, absorbing the surroundings.

"*Indeed, Mr Martel, Indeed. Everything on Orious is built with high precision and beauty......It's uniform, a standard we maintain throughout the planet unremittingly.....*"

After some time they reached the human quarters, driving down a long road, past the main intersection, colourful flowers and well pruned tress on either side. On a hill, a group of workers sprinkled water onto the soil, labouring away energetically. Beside them, an unusual looking animal munched on the grass, its great eyes half shut with fatigue. An elaborate white palace now came into view, compelling in its grandeur and innovative style.

"*We're here Jake,*" Ludovic whispered from the corner of his mouth. The decisive moment had come.

Inside the confines of the palace, they were escorted into a large office, meticulously arranged. From the white ceiling, an elegant chandelier hung. Through the windows, beams of sunlight filtered through, sparkling across the marble floor, the room reflected in its polished surface. The windows were wide, with heavy brass handles; somewhat odd for a world which had evidently kept up with the technocratic levels of the cosmos, and indeed, excelled in so many areas. Ludovic shook his head in disbelief as he caught a fleeting impression of the room.

"*Look Jake,*" he muttered quietly. "*They have anti-gravity technology at their disposal, yet they still open windows by hand....*"

"*Please gentlemen, take a seat...*" the Attaché said. "*Our leader will be with you in a moment......*"

Turning, he left, his footsteps fading into silence. They were now completely alone. Ludovic sat down and unzipped his folder, taking out the one document of vital importance....

"*We'll get this over with quickly......sharp and concise.*"

Jake winked, acknowledging mutely. A discreet smile passed across his face. Suddenly the doors opened.....the leader of Orious walked through imperially, dressed in a long grey cloak which slithered across the floor behind him....almost a mythological character. He was bald and clean shaven. His ancient eyes shone like two black pearls, ablaze with energy, an energy that appeared to consume the actual organ of sight itself. It went beyond the individual, beyond anything carnal.

His profound inner wisdom was displayed structurally across his face....it was reflected in his features. A strange thrill shot through them both, a deep sense of awe. Ludovic wondered why, devoid of an explanation.

"*Welcome....I'm Miryandis, Leader of Orious......*"

He sat on his chair, edging it closer to the desk. He spoke with great eloquence, his words spaced apart, yet powerful. It demanded acute attention. Almost immediately, the Leader of Orious sensed hostility, and with it, ripples of alarm.

"*Ludovic Martel, Earth Ambassador.*" He swallowed hard.

"*De Quent....Chief Scientist......*"

"*So gentlemen.......what brings you here with such urgency? I believe our two representatives have already established our standing in regards to the future of this planet.*"

Ludovic shuffled, adjusting himself.....his posture and facial expression unveiling the seriousness of his business.

"*Mr Miryandis.....I come here with strict orders....Please, if you will?*"

He pushed forward the legal document. A period of silence followed as Miryandis read rapidly, with muted urgency, controlling his expression throughout. The tension in the room was almost tangible. It mounted as the silence grew. Then......

"*So this is what it's come to?*" Realization dawned on him as he contemplated the devastating implications. He shook his head slowly.

"*Afraid so.....*" Ludovic replied.

"*Sir, you must understand one thing.....we control the systems throughout...we are the central source, implementing the laws and rules.....cultural trends and so forth.....Each solar system, each planet throughout the galaxy comes under one galactic hat.....one universal rule.......one way of living....Earth's way.....*"

Miryandis gazed at them silently.

"*It appears to me that you are devoid of certain facts. This planet, dear Sirs, is a very special planet, a jewel in space....As we have already stated, there is no way we will allow you to forcefully change our way of life......We have lived in peace and harmony for years......that won't alter......*"

"*Perhaps you don't understand,*" Jake said harshly. "*We have been authorised to blow you out of existence if you refuse to sign.....it's there in black and white......*"

"*So be it.....*"

Ludovic intervened. *"Are you honestly refusing to acknowledge us as the power here? For the sake of one simple signature you would rather cease to exist....killing billions of others in the process....in time your civilisation, this planet, will be nothing but a myth......a legend...a population of people wiped out of existence."*

"Indeed...maybe so," Miryandis muttered softly. *"But signing that document would bring this planet to an end regardless...only that it would be a slow gradual death..."*

"How do you mean?" Ludovic asked...forehead creased.

"Here on Orious we have our own laws which we adhere to rigorously....This has been the platform to our success. We alone have developed our own technology...created our own industries, our own methods......our own realities......For us to be ruled by you and come under the galactic hat......as you call it, is totally unacceptable......the changes would be radically negative...."

"But why...? Our methods are coherent, well thought out, full of integrated valid factors......controlled and maintained from a central source on Earth......And as for your position....it wouldn't be affected in the slightest......you would still govern the planet, under our guidance...under our law......"

"Mr Martel, there is no way......"

He rested his bare elbows upon the desk, pressing his hands together.

"Your laws are diametrically opposed to ours...they're based around control, an iron hand...people are not cattle....Here we place emphasis on love....we don't control nations using fear and brute force......we work on love....a rich and all consuming principal."

"Fear and force, Mr Miryandis...fear and force....humans understand no other way....it induces hate, anger, negative emotions......but it keeps a man alive. We have colonized the systems throughout adapting this methodology....."

Ludovic cut off.....sunlight streaming across his face.

"Hate, a sickness, highly contagious, spreads like a lethal virus......You have killed and waged war, stripped people of their will and dignity....nations, planets enslaved by the tyranny of fear. In startling contrast, our methods are founded on love......it's the only way....it conquers death and the fear of it. We will never accept your false ideologies that you impose......never..."

"Ideologies......" Jake blasted. *"Such as...?"*

"Atheism......"

The word ricocheted in his ears, flooding his body with rage. His mind reeled.

"*The galactic law is dominated by an atheistic philosophy, is it not? There is no way we could ever embrace it......death is better.*"

"*What!*" Jake snapped. "*How can you question fact? We are the product of evolution, nothing but animals, evolved monkeys......There is no Creator...*"

Ludovic interjected......

"*Just what is your problem with that?*"

"*Evolution, hmm......I'm afraid to tell you that it defies logic with perplexing irrationality, a totally specious theory, and even if for a moment we assumed it was the way all things came into being, what was the force behind such a highly complex process....things just don't self evolve ....accidentally....it would require a technician to have orchestrated it....would it not?*"

His voice was now filled with passion.....awe......

"*Man's existence is down to a Creator of supreme power, as are all the other complex life forms, such as animals, fish, and insects......But man is a very special creature, distinctly separate from any living thing. We humans are nothing short of a miracle......from the point of conception to birth, from a child to adulthood...in that life cycle there are clear miraculous progressive stages of change......growth, biological and chemical modifications, if you like, which are manifested externally, structurally......Is that all down to chance?......It is the human mind Gentlemen, a powerful electrochemical organ that sets us apart from any animal, any creature......the cerebral cortex....*"

They watched him apprehensively, shocked by his profound discourse.

"*In spite of all steadily accumulated knowledge, the mechanisms of the mind still remain a profound mystery......How could such an amazing organ develop on its own?*"

There was no answer......only confusion in the midst of such arguments.

"*Surely you must acknowledge the existence of a superior intellect. If I told you the ship that brought you here, just appeared from out of nowhere would you believe it? It required a designer, a builder, did it not? How much greater is the mind? Right now an incredible interchange of chemical and electrical activity is taking place in our head, breath-taking neurological activity...*"

Ludovic sat in agitated silence. Something deep within him had ignited; something he himself couldn't explain. The words rumbled through him poetically, causing him to reflect with reverence and growing enlightenment. He suppressed his reaction, masking it well. Miryandis continued.

"You see, the consequences of your philosophy stretch further than you could ever imagine......To live a life thinking that you are nothing but the product of a mistake......a bizarre series of collective unbalanced coincidences, will inevitably shape your persona....your daily approach, your morals, your view of the world and the people in it......negatively....of course. In your law book it states that an explosion set life into motion, thus creating everything that we see. Gentlemen, explosions destroy, they don't create......The facts are if you blow us out of existence, as you say you will....you won't come back to find another planet with life and people....Explosions cause chaos, disorder, disarray....no explosion could create this baffling orderly universe......and even if hypothetically speaking it was the case, it would still demand a technician to have planned it......"

"This is preposterous," Jake rumbled, his jaw jutting out in anger."

"Please allow me to finish and fully convey my message...."

Miryandis halted momentarily...

"Ask yourselves, what is the purpose of human life? It's such a short journey, and at times a painful one. We are very special, created for a purpose....a reason...."

"Which is?" queried Ludovic.

"Relationship......everything around us is about relationship. We see it in plants, insects, animals, and of course humans......There is a special interrelationship throughout the cosmos and beyond......without relationship we are nothing.....we need it in order to be certain of ourselves, our existence......and our place in the universe....."

Jake rose from his chair, his face a mask of rage, eyes cold with hostility. He interjected......

"You are living in a world of your own, Miryandis...."

"Yes indeed...and like that, it shall remain..."

"Mr Miryandis," Jake blasted icily. *"We haven't journeyed here for a theological debate...this is political......Are you saying that the only reason you refuse to sign is because theism is banned from our law...?"*

"Yes....yes indeed, but it appears to me that you are still failing to grasp what I'm saying......Your disbelief is the centre of the problem. It makes up the very foundation of your law......everything gravitates around it..."

Ludovic remained silent.

"Theism is the key to everything, the key to life, the very reason we are.....the very reason we exist......without it man dies...he is void, empty.....without a purpose, an

objective. We lose our way....our meaning, our identity.....We become dictator of what is right and wrong with a distorted subjective view.....We lose sight of our existence...our relationship with others.....with devastating consequences.....without it we are spiritually dead. It is the all essential component that is missing in your lives. To sign that document would mean death......Your faith gentlemen, is a weapon of destruction..."

"*Faith...? We have no faith Mr Miryandis....*"

"*Professor De Quent, to believe that this universe appeared out of nothing requires more faith than believing in a Creator....*"

"*Nonsense......?*"

"*How do you mean?*" Ludovic inquired meekly.

"*Let's use a basic mathematical formula to illustrate my point. Logical application is the key......Indulge me.....Nothing multiplied by nothing doesn't equate to everything, does it? Or in other words, out of nothing came everything.....everything in such order and beauty. But if you include a Creator into the equation it makes far more sense....*"

Jake's face hardened.

"*To the eye there is no absolute certainty either way, but when you apply logic....you realise that atheism requires far more faith than you could ever imagine, far more than theism.*"

Ludovic held a clenched fist to his mouth, eyes fixed.

"*But......but who created the creator?*"

"*God is and always will be. He is eternal. He is not bound by time. He is outside the sphere of time and space. He dwells in eternity....the Alpha and Omega. He can see the past, present and future in an instant. We who are locked in time cannot comprehend God's eternal being.....it is impossible. The eternality of God transcends science and human understanding... God simply is.....*"

A deafening silence fell......

"*The universe, my friends, is a marvel of order...immense, eternal and complex, filled with billions of galactic clusters....*

The human mind hasn't even begun to comprehend its mysteries.....Look at your solar system, your planet......Earth, one of the greatest cosmological scientific puzzles, confounding our efforts to understand it....it's where life all began, we are its descendants...a ball of clay filled with majestic colourful panoramas. It thrives with life and motion, sustained by very complex systems that provide, air, light, water and food in exquisite balance. As it orbits the sun once a year the Earth travels at an average speed of thirty kilometres per second......even its tilt allows for the seasonal changes.

Indeed life throughout the cosmos is characterized by this mind blowing arrangement....starting at an atomic level."

He stood, gazing towards the window....his eyes ablaze with energy, his face wise with profundity.

"*My friends, the universe demands a Creator of supreme power and intelligence......Everything around us is a living miracle.....from a microscopic organism.....to a human being.....*"

"*Mr Miryandis, you have a marvellously convoluted mind, but you are missing the whole point of this meeting.....Let's not degravitate from the point any further....*"

"*On the contrary dear Jake, please listen carefully, allow me to enlighten you further......We are nothing but a cluster of atoms...atoms are like miniature solar systems, forming covalent bonds due to a deficient amount of orbiting electrons, which in turn forms molecules......DNA...RNA strands, proteins the building blocks to life.....The cell, is like a miniature world of its own, a living factory alive with highly complex activity.....far more complex than anything known to man.....To fully understand what takes place in the nucleus of a cell is mind blowing......*"

Jake banged his fist against the desk, his face full of stubborn dignity.

"*That's enough......it ends here......sign or else!*"

"*Enough......?*" Miryandis replied piercingly, jabbing his finger towards him. Sudden authority stiffened his voice.

"*Yes, I'm sure Professor De Quent, sometimes the truth cuts so deep that only anger can rise up in an attempt to heal such a wound......but there is no repair, only acceptance....acceptance and the realization that we are imperfect beings in desperate need of change. The journey of life is like a grain of sand drifting through the ocean of time, swinging between a pendulum of life and death with an inevitable end. Our lives here will dictate our final fate, our final destination. It lies in our hands....*"

Ludovic looked over at Jake, almost conveying his inner conflicting emotions......growing bewilderment. Jake in turn remained focused, fuelled by loyalty and blind adherence to the law.

"*It's your choice Miryandis......you have decided your own fate.....with it a planet......*"

"*No De Quent, you are trapped, trapped in a state of cognitive dissonance and circular reasoning, the fundamental fallacy in logic......imprisoned by foolishness and delusions of grandeur......a warped mind. Your view of life is diametrically opposed to the truth. In order to attain the truth, you need to break free from the sphere of your own domain...*"

Seconds of silence passed......

"*I leave you with this: you may take our lives......you may destroy a race of people......a planet, but you will never kill the truth, never......*"

Back in the ship, far out afloat in space, Ludovic stood gazing at the slowly fading planet, his eyes deep and profound. The laser vaporizer had been set, its target Orious. Sitting beside the activator in his green luminous uniform was the military co-pilot, awaiting the vital command.

"*Sir......all set. We are just about at the right distance for activation....*" He looked through the target monitor, mapping out the precise location of impact......

Ludovic was still, ripples of sweat forming across his brow. The final words of Miryandis swept within him, echoing....tearing him apart. It had left all kinds of existential questions resonating in his mind. He was caught in a spiral of confused emotion.

"*Well,*" Jake grated from behind, seated in his revolving chair, tilting back, legs crossed.

"*Give the command. Soon Orious will be non-existent, nothing but a blazing mass of fire and ash......a few drifting rocks afloat in space......*"

He smirked, eyes cold as he pictured the destruction. The co-pilot sat rigidly......ready, finger on the activator......

"*Jake I......I can't......*"

He let it out in an unsteady rush of relief, running a shaky hand through his hair. Jake leapt to his feet......

"*What! Am I talking with Ludovic Martel...?*"

"*You heard me...I can't...*"

"*Have you lost your mind? What the heck has gotten into you......?*"

"*There are billions of people down there....children, families, humans...humans!*" He pointed with anguished concern. "*Who am I to take life? Who are we to decide the fate of a planet?*"

"*You, as the Ambassador, were given strict orders......you have two choices.....Either you comply or you face serious consequences...This won't be taken lightly. How could you allow that half crazed man to twist your mind?*"

"*Twist......? No Jake, he unlocked something within me, far more profound than what the material world can offer. His words were too eloquent, his logic wise and precise. An untamed wisdom that supersedes anything I've encountered...a master of dialectics. Man doesn't live forever...Who knows why we are here......who knows where*" *we are going? To dismiss these thoughts is total foolishness; they demand answers....To embrace atheism as truth is our biggest downfall. Our time here is almost nonexistent, a mere blink in the face of eternity. We get so caught up in the spiral of life that we seldom sit back and realise we are mortal beings with an end. The fear of death has always been our greatest enemy....the very knowledge of our own mortality. With certainty all life will cease.....and then......?"*

"And then what......?"

"Who knows Jake......Who knows......?"

Ludovic began walking towards the metallic passageway, his steps dragging as though depleted of energy. Suddenly he halted, turning, his hand pressed against the steel of the wall, his knuckles white. Both Jake and the co-pilot were motionless, mouths gaping in disbelief...

"I guess I'll have a lot of explaining to do when we get back......ugh...?"

He moved on, leaving nothing but silence in his trail except for the roar of the ship, as it continued its journey, piercing through the trackless void of eternity......

The Hidden Cave

Steering the speedboat to its maximum capacity, away from the fading coastline of San Francisco, with trained narrowed eyes, Pete Ellis turned and said, *"Just a couple of more kilometres and we'll stop......"*

Cliff Fontaine smiled in acknowledgment. Sitting rigidly in his wetsuit, he regulated his oxygen tank. A routine dive awaited him, one born out of adventure rather than necessity, the ocean luring him, a mysterious world; an ecosystem of its own.

Across the warm waters of the Pacific, darkness was now descending. Standing in his flippers, Cliff moved over towards Pete with controlled effort. There was no expression on his face, a stone-like detachment as he psyched himself up for the task at hand.

Easing the throttle, they came to a gradual halt, the engine ticking over quietly. The boat, now immobile, began to move and bounce gently. Engulfing them in all directions were miles of ocean water, dark and eerie. Above, the moon appeared large and luminous, casting its reflection over the face of the sea. A red warning light suddenly lit, flashing, signalling low fuel.

"Pete, I hope we have enough to get back......"

"Don't worry, it's an electrical malfunction......we've got plenty....." He switched off the engine.

Cliff's initial concern was nullified. As an eminent Marine Biologist and skilled scuba-diver, everything had to be done methodically. It was part of his character and of course fundamental to the line of work he was in. From the positioning of the stars, the sidereal cycle, the tides, and that inner sense of chronology, he guessed the hour then consulted his wrist-watch for confirmation. The glowing dials showed 21:00 hours.

"Okay......I'm ready," Cliff said brightly, making his final checks then tightening the strap of his buoyancy compensator around his waist. Moving to the edge of the boat, one step at a time maintaining equilibrium, he sat facing Pete.

"Give me fifty minutes......if I'm not up by then, you know what to do......"

Pete laughed......*"Hey come on, I'm sure the sharks have gotten used to you by now......"*

Before lowering his mask, Cliff winked and smiled......a smile full of confidence. The ocean, the darkness, and the feverish fears that came with his passion, never hindered him nor blocked that surging rush of excitement and hunger within. Focused and alert, he fixed the mask across his face, securing the demand valve around his gums. Then raising a thumb he fell backwards into the sea with a splash. All that was left on the surface was a pool of foam......bubbles, with it a deafening silence.

Descending into what looked like a cloudy abyss, he stretched out his left arm activating the torch with the click of a switch. Light refraction was a minor impediment, but he remained focused, solely dependant on the hazy beam of light which guided him further and further into the unknown. With a sharp twist of his body and a swift wiggle of his feet, he suddenly plunged down vertically, gaining rapid depth. The darkness grew, with it his adrenal fix and that inner hunger to explore the unknown. Reaching the sandy ocean bed of the Pacific, he halted in a fixed position and began moving the torch in a sideways motion. With poor visibility, all he could distinguish was a vast array of exotic looking corals. He felt at peace, away from the roar and commotion of the world.

Then unexpectedly, from out of nowhere, as if someone had turned on a switch, a light began emanating from what looked like a cave. Intrigued by what he saw, he began manoeuvring towards the entrance, almost as if magnetically attracted. This brilliant seemingly endless light had an extraordinary glow about it, alien-like. As he drew closer, he became totally absorbed in it. There was a sense of detachment, creating a dream-like effect beyond reality.

Slowly he entered, and was at once alerted to the fact that the light appeared to emanate out of nowhere. Turning and twisting, he couldn't comprehend from where it was coming. His discerning faculty had temporarily abandoned him. As a man of science, everything had to be based on logic.....not this time. This baffling phenomenon began to lure him in further, rather than repel him. A school of colourful fish suddenly shot past darting away into the distance, shattering his attention. As he breathed in his canned oxygen, he raised his wrist to the face of his mask to consult his watch. To his surprise it was malfunctioning, the dials spinning anticlockwise at great speed, nearly invisible to the eye. In a flash he felt faint, almost losing consciousness. He fought it, shaking his head vigorously; the blur and dizziness now beginning to fade. Gradually he regained composure and a steady thought pattern. Guided by survival instincts, he darted out of the luminous cave, and began a prompt controlled ascent.

The urge to escape the clutches of the ocean was mounting by the second; his ascent seemed to take an eternity. As he surfaced, there was a raging storm, waves tossing to and fro, rumbles of thunder echoing......lightening illuminating the sky dazzling white. Cold hard rain pelted down, the heavens dark and miserable, a thick grey cloud belt twisting and moving, concealing the night spheres. Within seconds he saw the boat, and the dim figure of Pete waving over. The wind picked up speed, howling and swishing around without respite.

"*Pete,*" he cried, the demand valve stifling his voice, the muffled tones vibrating through his facial bones and mask.

In a quick burst, Cliff swam his way over battling through the oncoming ice-cold waves. It was testing, but he fought through until he reached the side of the boat. Instantly, Pete knelt down lowering his hand in support.

"*Steady......*" he gasped, the cords in his neck rippling with tension and strain.

Grasping Pete's outstretched hand, Cliff climbed aboard, sliding the mask from his face. Pulling the demand valve from his mouth, he coughed. His normal breathing pattern was rapidly restored.

"*Are you okay Cliff? The weather just took a turn......it's getting pretty bad....we'll have to head back immediately......*"

"*Pete, wait, listen......I had the most bizarre experience down below......*"

Pete was silent......curious.

"*There was a light......a bright light coming from a cave.....it just happened all of a sudden......*"

"*Are you serious......did you investigate?*"

"*Yeah......but......*"

"*But what......?*"

The storm began to worsen, rocking the boat violently, causing loose equipment to slide around on deck, some plunging overboard.

"*I think we'd better make headway......*"

"*Guess so,*" Cliff replied his voice dull and strained, his face filled with bewilderment.

With the roar of the engine, they commenced their journey back to shore, bouncing and dipping over the face of the angered sea.

"Cliff......Cliff honey wake up, it's almost twelve......"

Opening his dark fatigued eyes, sleep began to dissolve, the cream coloured ceiling and the world around him coming into focus. In the background he could hear the radio, the usual morning dose of Country and Western resonating dimly in his ears. Blindly he threw his hand in its direction lowering the volume into silence.

"Cliff," his wife said again, now capturing his attention... *"Are you ever going to give me a moment of your time....? You and the ocean......never a moment for us..."*

His wife stood there peering over at him closely, her hand resting at her hip awaiting a reply. He stretched out his hand tugging her towards him. Pulled over by his grip, the bed gave way due to the sudden additional weight.

"Sandy babe..." He smiled playfully, now fully alert to his surroundings. *"This compulsion and obsession of mine has given us a lavish lifestyle.....one which you seem to enjoy..."*

He cupped her chin in the palm of his hand, gazing into her eyes. They kissed, an intimate kiss, warm and tender. At that moment, the door swung open, halting halfway. Billy rushed in, red cheeked, chocolate smudged across his lips and striped vest.

"Daddy," he cried in his squeaky voice, jumping across the bed into his father's reassuring arms.

"Hey little man.....no school today...?"

"Cliff, it's a holiday," his wife replied fixing her heavy mass of golden hair in the mirror."

The phone rang, shattering the warm family atmosphere. Sandy lifted the receiver.

"Honey, it's Pete...."

She walked over handing him the phone, leaving the room immediately, Billy following mischievously behind.

"Hey Cliff, how's it going....?"

"Okay I guess." He yawned, eyes shut. *"Just here with the family, but still none the wiser as to last night's strange underwater encounter....That light, that cave......and that's not all......"*

He frowned as he recaptured the moment.

"*Oh yeah that's right,*" Pete replied brightly, "*I mentioned it to Brad this morning.....*"

"*Brad......Brad who?*"

"*Brad Stevens......who else?*"

Cliff was puzzled....

"*Pete......I don't know Brad Stevens.*"

"*Are you joking......? You've known him for more than ten years......*"

A moment of hesitation......

"*Cliff, are you certain you're okay?*"

Cliff clung tighter to the phone, mute and immobile, broken dream-like thoughts and theories racing through his mind......

"*In answer to your question.....it all depends on whether you're being serious......Pete,*" his voice grew in pitch tinged with an element of annoyance, "*I don't know any Brad....*"

"*Wait......are you honestly saying you have no knowledge or recollection of him?*"

"*Yes, that's precisely what I'm saying......*"

Pete's concern grew......

"*Look buddy, I don't know what happened to you last night, but it appears you've suffered some kind of memory loss...the implications to what you encountered may be vast....I think we need to talk.....I'll come by right away....*"

As the call ended, Cliff was lost in a haze of worry and confusion. Placing the phone on the bed, he made his way to the door, pausing at the spiral staircase. After seconds of contemplation, he headed to the kitchen where Sandy stood washing a stack of dirty dishes. Instantly she realised something was wrong.

"*Babe......you okay?*"

"*Not sure......*"

He scratched his head nervously, seating himself at the breakfast table, trying to regain composure, the bright kitchen lights demarking clearly his thought drenched features.

"*I don't understand,*" she replied, "*Not sure about what?*"

"*Tell me.....do we know a Brad Stevens? Or perhaps I should rephrase it......do I know a Brad Stevens?*"

His mystified eyes grew wide as he looked at her, almost willing her to say no. Sandy walked over and sat beside him, puzzled......taken aback by the question.

"*Cliff honey, are you serious?*"

"*Evidently so......*"

An interval of silence......

"*Babe......we've known Brad and Sally-Anne Stevens over ten years now......why are you asking me such a stupid question?*"

His face lit with panic, his jaw rigid, teeth locked.....

"*Sandy, it's because I have never met this person, nor do I have any recollection of him......or in fact, them...*"

"*Cliff stop......you're scaring me....*"

At that moment the door bell rang, breaking the tense atmosphere....

"*I'll get that,*" Sandy said walking away anxiously.

Minutes later, Pete stepped into the kitchen, Sandy following behind...

"*Hi Cliff, how are you feeling...?*"

"*Pete listen to me....I know what you are thinking, but please believe me, I'm not suffering from a neurological disorder.....nor am I suffering from memory loss.*"

Pete walked over and sat facing him, Sandy motionless in the corner.

"*What Cliff, what are you suggesting then?*" He crossed his legs leaning back, eyeing him analytically.

"*I don't know myself......*"

"*Cliff this is bizarre, totally bizarre. Brad has been your dear friend for the last ten years, do you honestly have no recollection of him at all?*"

Cliff didn't answer.....instead he began to stare at the surroundings with a cold hard expression on his face. Oddly everything around him seemed different, tiny details like the positioning of the breakfast table, the ambience, the flowery scent in the air. He was engulfed by a number of peculiarities; the fear was minor in comparison to his awareness of the baffling predicament he was in.

"*What is it, Cliff?*" Pete asked abruptly, jerking him out of his daze. Sandy approached, her face pallid......anxious.

"*There, that picture...that picture above the sink....I don't recall that being there......*"

"*Sweetheart, it's been there ever since we moved in five years ago.*"

She eyed Pete with penetrating alarm. He acknowledged her bewilderment and returned the same mystified stare.

"*Cliff, are you saying you don't recall that picture......?*"

"*No Pete, I remember the picture alright, but I don't recall it being located there......In fact we had it hanging upstairs, in the bedroom....*"

He pointed to affirm that was indeed the case, although deep down, he was beginning to question his sanity.

"*Look, I think you should get some rest......tomorrow morning I'll have an appointment booked......*"

Before he could finish, Cliff interrupted. "*With whom Pete...? A psychiatrist...?*"

He paused......

"*It's as if......*"

"*Go on,*" Sandy urged with wide apprehensive eyes, holding onto his shoulder.

"*It's as if there's a distinct barrier between me and this......this reality......this world. Damn!*" he yelled leaping to his feet, his face filled with ripples of tension.

Walking over to the sink he halted, frozen to the spot and stood gazing through the window towards the still, quiet sidewalk. Then, with a submissive acceptance, he held his hand to his forehead...

"*This is futile.....Sandy, call Doctor White, see if you can fix me an urgent appointment......*"

Without replying, she ran into the corridor and sprang towards the phone......

At the Doctor's Surgery, Cliff was called over by the receptionist. It was his turn to see Dr White. As he stood there, Sandy tugged his jacket....

"*Shall I come in with you?*"

"*No, it's ok, don't worry....*"

He forced a broken washed out smile, a bold attempt to allay Sandy's growing fears. As transparent as it was, it gave her a flicker of hope, something to hold onto.

Slowly, he made his way over, halting by the reception desk, where a neat looking brunette directed him through. Inside the Doctor's office,

Cliff slumped into a brown leather chair. The Doctor adjusted his tie and began.

"*So Professor Fontaine......how can I help?*"

There was no immediate reply, just a long extended exchange of calculated glances.

"*Sorry Doc, I just don't know how to convey this to you without your instantly assuming that I'm suffering from some kind of neurological disorder......*"

"*Let me be the judge of that......*"

A brief pause......

"*This morning, whilst in discussion with a dear friend and colleague, he mentioned someone, a person....a person that I have never heard of, nor had any kind of interaction with for that matter......when I told him I had never known him, this left him stunned....bewildered...*"

"*Why......?*" the Doctor inquired, keen interest in his voice.

"*Why? It's because......*" He began to fidget and clasp his hands tightly..."*It's because he claims I know him...for over ten years now, and that's not all...my wife Sandy agrees with him....*"

"*Extraordinary...Tell me, have you had any other strange encounters......? I mean anything equally bizarre as what you just told me?*"

"*No, not exactly, but there are other things......For example, in the kitchen, hanging over the sink is a picture.....but that picture was never there, I know it for a fact.*"

"*Where was it then?*"

"*Hanging in the bedroom...When I told my wife, she was adamant that it had been there ever since we moved in......five years ago...but I tell you that's not the case....*"

"*Sir, these are a strange series of delusions, from your medical records you have never suffered from any type of psychological problem. To assume that you are now is clearly not the case.....you are so rational and coherent in your approach and explanation.....your mind, lucid...*"

"*So what's happening to me then?*"

"*Memory loss, temporary memory loss....at this stage it's the most probably diagnosis.....*"

He halted, absorbed in profound thought.

"*Tell me, have you been under any stress lately....or can you think of anything that may have triggered off this possible condition?*"

For the first time since his strange underwater encounter, Cliff began to wonder whether or not there was some kind of connection. *'How and why?'* he questioned, fishing futilely for answers, but to no avail. Yet something told him deep inside there was indeed a link. At least chronologically it all seemed to add up. *'What was that light?'* he thought pensively. *'From where did it come....?'*

"Doc.....last night I was diving......"

"Yes......"

"And then....." Cliff broke off and swallowed hard, as if searching for the correct words to use. *"A strange light,"* his voice rose as he pictured it......*"There was this strange light emanating from an underwater cave......it happened all so suddenly."*

Intrigued, the Doctor sat up straight, putting his fingers to his lips.

"Please continue......"

"As I entered, the light source appeared to shine from out of nowhere......"

"Were you alone the whole time?"

"Yes, yes I was......"

"What occurred next?"

"My watch started malfunctioning, the dials spinning at great speed....then I almost lost consciousness.....As a vastly experienced diver, I have never encountered such a phenomenon, it's as if......as if it came from another world..."

Struck by his own words, he suddenly paused. Images and metaphysical theories began flashing through his mind, accompanied by a foreboding sensation until it had become a fully blown revelation.

"Another world being the operative word," he said under his breath, barely moving his lips.

"What was that?"

"Thanks Doc, that'll be all."

Cliff leapt up, heading for the door. Despair cut through him. His pulse altered....his stomach knotting.

"Professor Fontaine, please......"

It was no use, he was gone, the sound of his hurrying footsteps dying off. The Doctor stood, biting his lip, pensive and puzzled.

On the way home, Cliff sat fixed to the passenger seat, gazing at the stars as if he found refuge in them, gripping onto something he could clearly identify and familiarize himself with. Across from him, in the silence, Sandy sat; her trim shape and pretty features faintly visible in the gloom. She looked anxious, preoccupied.

"*Cliff, you should not have left like that. You just stormed out of there like a crazed man......*"

"*Sandy, please......don't let me repeat myself....*"

Ahead, the beaming lights of a passing truck swept into the car, breaking the flow of the heated discussion. Its engine groaned and rumbled noisily. It was now behind them, descending down the road, away into the distance.

As they arrived, the outside house lights activated, filtering through the vine-entangled doorway entrance and reflecting against the hood of the car. He flung the door open and stepped out into the zone of light, lifeless leaves crunching under the weight of his feet. A few drifted past him, guided, tossed by the wind into the vast cloud of night. By the foyer, the weather beaten rocking chair creaked. The night chill brought with it a wind which swished around, almost pulling him in the direction of the door. Entering the dimly lit hallway, Billy came rushing over in his green pyjamas, wild joy leaping through him.

"*Mommy, Daddy...*"

"*Hi Mrs Fontaine,*" the nanny said stepping out from the kitchen, her old wrinkled face alive and chirpy. "*He's just finished supper, time for homework...*"

"*You heard Ms Watson Billy, off you go.*"

Bending she kissed him, and then with a pat and rub on the head, little blond Billy darted off, dashing up the stairs almost losing his footing.

"*Thanks Ms Watson......*"

"*Pleasure mam.....Just give me a call whenever needed, a day's notice preferably......*"

In the library under a bright table lamp, Cliff sat leafing through a series of history books. Across the tiled floor a shadow emerged; it broke his focus temporarily.

"*Cliff what are you doing?*"

"*Reading......*"

As if crazed, he continued leafing through the pages feverishly, fingering his way around sentences which seemed to tamper with his already broken and confused state of mind. Then, in swift motion, he leapt to his feet.

"*Sandy, listen to me...I know what I'm about to say may sound crazy, I also know that I'm not suffering from memory loss, in fact, I have a clear vivid recollection of the past 30 years....*"

He sat back down, running a shaky hand through his hair.

"*It now appears there are other things which don't make any sense......Even historical events are not the way I recall them......Tell me......who is Clark O'Donnell?*"

There was an astonished silence, enough to detect the flicker of a heartbeat.

"*Are you seriously asking me that?*"

"*Yes......*"

"*Why, he is the president of the United States and has been for sometime......*"

"*Never heard of him......Tell me,*" he paused regaining his breath. "*Was there a Vietnam war?*"

"*What war....?*"

He stood abruptly, walking over to her.

"*Sandy don't you see there was a war, it did happen. March 8 1965, the first U.S. combat troops arrived in Vietnam.....and as for this O'Donnell.....why I haven't even heard of him...... *"

His face began to contort in horror. Sandy stood motionless.

"*Cliff, I think you need to see someone right away....*"

"*No Sandy, I don't need a Doctor....Deep beneath the sea lies a gateway to another world, another dimension, one parallel to our own. In that light flooded cave I somehow stumbled into it....into this reality......*"

"*I can't believe this......You're insane, totally insane......*"

She broke down, tears burning in her eyes. Reaching over, he held her in his arms.....but with a stern shrug, she freed herself from his grip and headed away towards the lounge, helpless and afraid.

It was now morning. A new day approached. As the door bell rang, Cliff awoke, raising his head stiffly from his library desk. At once, the reality of his predicament penetrated. Again the door bell rang, followed by a knock. Bewildered and torn, he made his way over, and from the corner of his eye caught a quick glimpse of Sandy standing quietly midway up the spiral staircase, Billy close by. Swinging the front door open, sunlight flooded in, stinging his eyes, breaking his morning drowsiness......

"Hi Cliff......I've brought a friend...."

Standing before him was Pete, accompanied by a man dressed in a long dark coat and blue shirt.

"May we come in?"

Cliff's instinctive reaction was to keep silent. But after a few seconds he nodded his head. Instantly Pete stepped in, the unknown man followed, shutting the door behind him.

"Cliff......this is Brad......Brad Stevens...."

"Hi Cliff, how are you?" Brad said smiling, gazing at him in sympathetic concern, as if confronting a sick man. Cliff immediately understood the implication from Brad's transparent gesture and tone. Brad then reached out his hand in greeting, but Cliff failed to respond.

"I'm sorry I don't know you......nor do I have any recollection of you......none......"

Brad's smile dropped.

"There's no point in this, Pete......I'm telling you, I have never met this man......and if you want an explanation, I have one, as incredulous as it may seem..."

"Yes that's right...Sandy told me about your theory..."

"Not a theory Pete, fact. But I'm looking for a solution, a way out of here, back into my world......"

Pete and Brad glanced at each other with worried eyes. Sandy began to inch her way down the stairs, Billy holding onto her anxiously.

"Cliff, listen to me, forget metaphysics, you need medical attention, you are suffering from some kind of neurological condition, a psychotic phase. Stop with this parallel dimension nonsense!"

"No Pete......hear me out......Do I sound like a mad man? Does a mad man speak with such depth, and clarity....? That cave, that light catapulted me into an alternate dimension, a parallel dimension, some kind of space time continuum. As I can see, most things around are largely the same, us, streets......but..."

"But what......?"

"But there are differences.....like this man Brad. In my world he doesn't exist, at least not to my knowledge......in addition to that, it appears to me that even historical events which I know took place, never occurred here, or if they did, it was somehow different.....I spent all night researching...."

"Such as..."

"*Such as the Vietnam War, it happened alright but the history books don't even mention it.....it is nowhere to be found, no record of it whatsoever.....and as for O'Donnell being the president, never even heard of him! Even the Great Roman Empire, the very one which shaped and built Europe, and transformed our way of thinking for all ages, according to what I read, never existed.....Great famous scientists that made earth shattering inventions are nowhere to be found, and are substituted by others which I know never lived......*"

"*Like......?*"

"*Like Enrico Fermi, who started the atomic age......according to the encyclopaedia it was Edward Wilson an American from Washington......list after list of things that just don't add up......a continuity of events that no memory loss could cause....nor any mental illness for that matter......I know what I know......In these parallel realities there are differences, some tiny, others major but there are differences.....This mysterious dark universe is so complex, made up of atoms....sub-atomic particles, strings of light oscillating with a frequency of which we are all part......a symphony of sounds within a multiverse of parallel dimensions, infinite realities...*"

"*Cliff, listen to yourself,*" Brad said. "*Are you suggesting that the Cliff Fontaine that stands before me, before us...is not the one we have known all these years?*"

"*Yes, correct......Don't you see that logic would indicate that to be so, there is no other explanation....Clearly you can see that I'm not insane......*"

"*So if that's the case, where is your counterpart?*" Pete asked, as if he had now succumbed to the theory. "*Where is the other you....?*"

"*I don't know......perhaps in my world....perhaps in another, who knows, but that's not my problem......If there is a way back, my only chance is to relocate that cave......?*"

"*Stop it......will you stop,*" Sandy cried tearfully. Then impulsively, she ran up the stairs, Billy trailing behind.

In the silence that followed, Cliff began to feel an element of guilt rising within him, but logic told him to push it aside, after all, these people were not who they appeared to be. He meditated, grasping it in its totality, even though he still questioned his sanity. Walking off into the library he sat at his desk, nervous sweat breaking out on his forehead. Moments later he heard the front door open and close, then footsteps approaching. Pete stepped in, sunlight shining across his body as it filtered in through the elegantly curtained window.

"*Talk to me Cliff......Brad's gone, it's just you and me.....*"

"*What more is there to convey? I'm from another world, one where there is another Pete Ellis, one where there's another Sandy and Billy......one where I belong......*"

His voice faded. Calmly, Pete walked over, and knelt beside him. There was a warm expression on his face, one of acceptance, as if his whole trail of thinking had now switched. Cliff captivated it with a glance.

"*Cliff, I don't know why......but a part of me is beginning to believe you....yet another is telling me you need urgent help. Emotionally I'm being pulled, torn in two separate directions, but because of our friendship, because of my respect for you...as ludicrous as it is......*"

He paused, his eyes straying away from Cliff towards the floor, conveying the dilemma he was in.

"*We're going back.....back out there. If what you're saying is the case, we have no other choice but to find that cave......*"

Cliff stood up, and walked towards the window where the growing light of day revived him with hope.

"*It's my only hope Pete......my only hope......*"

As darkness approached, they commenced their journey across the tame Pacific waters. Accelerating to maximum speed, Pete navigated ahead in search of the precise location......

"*I'm doing my best to relocate the exact spot of your dive, but you do realise it may not be possible......?*"

Beside him, dressed in his wetsuit, Cliff remained quiet, solely focused on his objective, one which hung in the balance. After all there was no guarantee he could ever escape the clutches of this other world......

"*Okay,*" Pete said, "*this will do, it was around here somewhere......*"

Cliff was unresponsive as he moved over to the side of the boat, staring into the cold waters of the Pacific, trance-like.

"*Cliff......*"

Turning slowly, he gazed at Pete who stood in a luminous yellow jacket. For a time there were no words, yet the muted urgency was plain to see.

"*Cliff.....as bizarre as it is......I hope you make it back......*"

"*Me too, Pete......me too....*"

Securing the demand valve around his gums, he bit hard into the rubber activating his diving torch. Then, with a sharp twist he jumped into the sea, rocking the boat, vanishing below......

Seconds of blackness passed, then light, bright and fiery engulfed him. In a flash, he found himself staring at his watch inside the cave, the light pulsing and glowing around him as if it were alive. For a brief moment he fought to maintain consciousness, as the whole scene was almost too much for him to fathom. Briskly, with snake-like motion he swam out, making a quick yet controlled ascent. With his torch his only guide, he could now see the surface drawing closer, the night stars coming into gradual but blurry focus. Pushing a little harder with the aid of his flippers, he was out, out with a splash, sapped dry and lifeless yet his adrenal fix remained. Locating Pete, he attempted to swim over with a series of breast stroke motions, but he couldn't. He paused, solely dependant on his buoyancy compensator to stay afloat.

"*Cliff, hold on buddy....*" Pete yelled, manoeuvring the boat cautiously in his direction.

Cliff's eyes began to close as he gazed up towards the sky in search of refuge. Barely conscious, he caught a glimpse of Pete as he reached out his desperate arms from beyond the boat. But which Pete was it?

A dazzle of light awoke him, as the Doctor shone a pencil beam torch into his left eye. He flinched and leapt up acting on impulse, sweating profusely, the dim bed lamp casting a shadow across his sickly face.

"*Where am I?*"

"*It's okay now*," the Doctor said warmly. "*You're at home, safe.*"

Cliff lay back, soaking up sweat from his face with his pyjama sleeve. Then, from the doorway, Sandy walked over, her face coming into focus as it met with the dim light of the bedroom. Slowly, reaching out, she held his hand, delicately kneeling beside the bed, her warm perfume filling his nostrils.

"*Baby, are you okay?*"

"*What......what happened......?*"

"*You were out diving with Pete.....don't you recall? You lost consciousness as you surfaced....*"

"*Yes, that's right*," he replied softly, barely moving his lips, Sandy's words acting as a catalyst, to restore his thought process. Gradually, he began to condense his fractured thoughts and broken memories into a semblance of logic. Then, at once, he recalled his predicament....

"*Light.....that light....*"

Sandy stood gazing at the Doctor, as if in need of support.

"*Light....what light? What do you mean?*" she asked, now staring at Cliff.

The Doctor promptly intervened.

"*It's okay Mrs Fontaine, he's probably delirious...rationality at this stage isn't expected......In a few days he'll be back on his feet, stronger and fitter than ever......*"

"*Thanks Doctor White......Can I see you out?*"

"*No, I'll be okay......if you need anything just call.*"

Offering a firm handshake, he smiled, transmitting an element of courage into her. Swiftly, with briefcase in hand, he left......

Making her way over to the bed, she stood gazing at Cliff worriedly. He still appeared dazed, yet mentally he was piecing together the chain of events like a puzzle. The one vital question that now remained was, had he made it back? The reaction of his wife indicated so, but there was only one real way to find out.

"*Sandy, I need to ask something....Please listen to me...*"

"*Sweetheart, calm down. Let me fix you some hot tea...Give me a couple of minutes......*"

Now quiet and alone, he gazed around the room almost hoping for some kind of indication, an indication that he was back in his world. Suddenly, the warm silence was shattered by the phone ringing. Reaching over he answered, low and strained..."*Yes....*"

"*Hey Cliff, it's Pete....are you feeling better....? You don't know how relieved I am to hear your voice. I was worried, man.....*"

For a moment Cliff hesitated, rubbing his hand across his bristled chin. Calculating his words carefully, he replied.

"*Yes, I'm feeling okay......but whether I remain that way depends.....*"

"*Depends on what?*"

"*Pete, I need to ask you two questions....*"

"*Go ahead....*" he said with curiosity....

"*Tell me.....*" Cliff's eyes began to switch from left to right, as if he were about to discover the ultimate truth. He took a long deep breath and continued......

"*Do I know a Brad Stevens......?*"

"*Who's Brad Stevens......?*"

Cliff was filled with relief.....

"*Pete......I know it sounds strange, but let me finish....Second question.......was there a Vietnam War...?*"

Pete chuckled to himself......"*Yes Cliff there was, it lasted many years....Now are you going to tell me what this is all about....?*"

"*I don't know how to put this......what I'm about to say may shock you......Deep beneath the sea, deep beneath the ocean I found a cave......*"

"*So......*"

"*And it was like no other....There was a light, a light which shone from it......a light from no apparent source.....*"

"*And......*"

"*Pete, somehow in this cave I stumbled into another world......another dimension.....a parallel dimension, one almost identical to this....in that dimension I lived out two days......*"

"*What......? Are you serious....?*"

"*Please, you've got to believe me......*"

"*Cliff, I'm sure there's a rational explanation behind it....Remember you were unconscious for some time......*"

"*No Pete, it happened......It was real......*"

There was a moment of silence....

"*Look, this is all a bit bizarre...for now try and get some much needed rest.....We'll speak again in the morning.....okay?*"

"*Okay Pete.....*"

Tossing the phone across the bed, Cliff caught the muffled tones of a young girl. Instantly he thought of his son Billy. '*Where was he?*' Sudden panic besieged him....The door swung open. She ran over......

"*Daddy....!*"

Terra Unknown

In the mid-day sky, a great shattering roar filled the air, a circle of light sparkling across the planet as they manoeuvred for descent. From the rocket-ship, exhaust valves gushed out clouds of smoke as the jet compressors cooled into silence. Via vocal instruction the hatch door slid open, making contact with the unknown world. Greg Myers, Commander, stepped out, dirt and ash blowing across the view plate of his helmet, his heavy tank weighing him down. Behind, two troopers followed, their grey pressurized gravity-suits glinting in the light.

"*What do you think Commander....as expected?*"

"*Yes.....definite signs of some sort of past existence......we've had this planet under observation for sometime...but now there's no doubt....*"

He pointed towards the lifeless landscape, death....ruins everywhere, buildings broken down and half burnt; yellowing remains of structures jutting up from the ground. Across the sky, dark rolling clouds of blackness covered the horizon, grey particles rising and falling. A sombre oppression hung over everything. Around his wrist the rad-detector registered and clicked. Greg consulted it, taking its atmospheric reading.

"*This planet is riddled with radiation......a sign that there may have been a war here......Unreal, how could any civilisation blast themselves out of existence?*"

All three looked ahead in silence; desolation and destruction everywhere.

"*Doug......*" He motioned him forward.

"*Yes Commander...?*" he said lowering the temperature of his suit, kicking debris and rubble from his path.

"*Radio in.....tell them we've finally made contact......Some believed we would never make it....*"

Harris began to fidget nervously, his heavy boots sinking into the dirt below.

"*Commander, are we safe here?*"

Greg hesitated, peering into the distance through the rising mist, Harris following his gaze.

"*That's something I can't answer right now....that's the chance we take each mission.....*"

Harris ran his fingers over his cased blast-gun, drawn by a sense of doom. Kneeling, Doug activated the transmitter from across his belt, blowing sharply against the mike. There was a hum then static....followed by a voice, cold, distant and metallic......

"Alpha-3 do you copy? Hello Alpha-3....."

Only faint crackling sounds were now audible....

"Commander I've lost them...."

"Don't worry we'll make contact once we're back inside the ship, the communications circuit should be fully operative......"

Greg considered....

"Amazing.....our calculations were spot on. This planet is roughly the same size as ours......the gravity field is ideal....The escape velocity will almost be the same as when we left our planet. I knew there would be life...at least there once was......"

He smiled to himself with satisfaction....

"Before we leave we need to activate the suction discs....we have to take back a tank full of atmosphere for testing... "

Overhead a winged creature flew past, circling for a time.

"Hey, did you see that......?" Harris rasped, pointing.

Greg gazed up, focusing, watching it go. *"I'm sure there are all sorts of living things here. Things beyond our wildest imagination....things which have become immune to the lethal radiation....Any creature alive is obviously well adapted to the environment......the levels of radioactivity are deadly.....practically nothing should exist...... "*

To the left something shone. Greg knelt, investigating, the others shielding around him.

"What is it?" Doug asked....rivulets of sweat forming, dripping down the inside face of his helmet.

"A chronological instrument....a device for measuring time..."

Harris's eyes widened.

"Okay, let's head into the rocket-ship," Greg said in his deep voice. He stood up, dusting his knees. *"We need rest....we've had quite a journey. Tomorrow we'll begin our search...we'll cover a six mile radius, beyond that..."* He paused.

"Beyond that what, Commander...?" Harris questioned.

"Who knows.....who knows......"

They turned gazing towards the desolate expanse...the poisonous wind lashing and twisting endlessly across the face of the planet like a tempest.....and silence...the eternal silence......

The next morning they were four kilometres out from base, Harris waving his scan-com every now and then, in search of alien spy ships. Off to the left a great gaping cavity stretched, deep and dusty. Greg trudged over through the rubble, halting near the edge, analysing, wondering. From his gloved hand a light shone as he raised it directing his palm towards the hole. He could see electronic equipment, weapons and highly advanced machinery, grey and bulky. A few creatures rustled and moved; vague indistinguishable shapes in search of refuge.

"*What is it?*" Doug inquired leaning over his broad shoulder, blast-gun in hand.

"*It seems to be some kind of underground quarters....From what I see nothing worth exploring......*"

"*Are you certain?*"

"*Yes.....besides, it won't be easy getting down there.....*"

A machine hummed, partially operating, a complex pattern of lights flashing and alternating with endless combinations. Doug calmly fired at it, a burst of heat blasting out, bursting it apart, springs and components spraying in all directions. He fired again through the mist of particles.

"*That should fix it......*"

"*Commander...!*" Harris yelled. "*I can see smoke in the distance.*"

Through parting mist a fire burned, thick dark smoke ascending.

"*Can you see it? There must be someone out there......*"

"*Could be...*" Greg replied unlatching his cased blast-gun, eyes focused. Silently he made a forward command, raising his hand and waving it in a circular motion......

Trudging through the ash with slow calculated steps, they advanced. Then something moved, a furry creature concealing itself in the rubble. Harris fired instinctively, his stomach turning, a wave of heat blasted into the atmosphere.

"*Damn I missed.....*"

The air was filled with an acrid stench. Again it moved, hopping away in a flash.

"*Look at it go.*" Greg said, "*A complex bundle of amino acids......nothing more......*"

Doug grimaced, imprisoned within the confines of his helmet. The smell of perspiration grew. He turned a dial across his chest regulating the temperature flow of his suit.

"*I don't think I can last another moment cooped up in this suit...it's torturing....*"

"*Come, let's push on,*"...Greg ordered....

Reaching the fire, everything was still, nothing stirred, only sporadic crackles; smouldering fragments. Harris gazed around scanning the landscape, no sound, no motion. He could almost smell his own fear which cut through him like a knife. Ahead on the horizon, he could see a range of mountains, a few rays of sunlight lighting their peaks. Greg spoke, severing the silence.

"*This must have been a small town, look, demolished structures everywhere......*"

A line of wrecked buildings stretched into the distance. In the centre of the street the ground caved in, its surface covered in stones, and broken glass. A few weeds and plants grew from the ground, multi-coloured blossoms; signs of some kind of remaining life.

"*Commander....what kind of civilisation lived on this planet?*

We haven't seen any evidence of the previous inhabitants.....nothing but semi-archaeological remains...if that..."

"*The war must have occurred sometime ago Harris......all that's left of them is probably organic matter......dust......*"

"*I wonder what they looked like, their physiology, their biological make-up, cell structure, digestive system. Radically different from ours I'm sure...Fascinates me.....What are the chances of finding any alive?*"

"*None.....*"

"*You don't sound optimistic Commander.....*"

There was no reply. A wind began screeching around them spraying dust into the air. The fire flickered feebly, fading slowly. Harris picked up a rusted pipe and began stirring it. The fire hissed spraying sparks around him.

"*Hey, look at these long stalks,*" Doug exclaimed, running his hand around one, assessing. "*Some kind of plant life....*" It was hard and coarse, like sandpaper, its leaves dripped with slime. "*Who knows, it may be edible...but then again I wouldn't chance it.....*"

The day wore on......hours passing. They were way out. Ahead stood a large building amazingly untouched, a hard looking structure with no signs of damage. There were no windows, only a door, grey and distinct. Halting in their steps, Greg pondered......

"*Strange, the one and only structure still standing in its entirety....must be of importance, built from special alloys......Perhaps bomb proof...*"

Greg walked over alone, trudging cautiously until he reached the building. Fatigue set in, his legs burned with lactic acid, stiffening. With a heavy hand he pushed at the door, but it wouldn't budge.....Then, reaching for his blast-gun he moved back a few steps and fired. The door stood firm, repelling the impact. Finally, he activated his laser-torch, in an attempt to burn through it. Again, it stood firm.

"*Doug....Harris,*" he yelled. "*I'll have to use a D-Bomb.....this door won't open......*"

Moving back at a set distance, Greg unfastened a disc from his belt, unscrewing the cap and locking it into place. Squatting, with a wave he signalled to the others to take position. They knelt, heads down, eyes closed. Greg calculated the trajectory, gazing at the door, his face tense, his mind focused. Then in swift motion, he threw the disc-bomb. It sailed through the air, hitting the ground, bouncing and rolling until it halted beside the target. Suddenly, it exploded, blowing the door apart. A wave of hot air rushed over their heads, shrapnel flying in all directions, dust and ash. Underfoot faint vibrations shot through the ground, but apart from the door, the structure stood, absorbing the aftershock. They waited watching the dust fade. The door was gone, dissolved into particles.

Suddenly a robot leapt out from the clouds of ash, its mechanical photocell eyes yellow and luminous. Swiftly, Harris opened his blast-gun, slid a fresh round of ammunition into place, snapped it shut and pointed. Running his finger over the trigger he stood firm.....methodically took aim and fired. The beam connected, blowing the robot apart, wires, springs, and circuits flying into the air. All activity from it ceased, its luminous eyes fading, winking until there was no movement. Its elongated steel jaw hung open, exposing tiny intricate components.

Greg immediately walked over, the others following behind. Standing over it he knelt, studying it intently, prodding into the gaping beam hole across its chest. Although inert, tiny wheels continued to spin, miniature components labouring, feebly operating. With a finger he touched the motor circuit. Its half blown arm swung aside.

"*This is one complex bundle of machinery, very similar to the ones constructed back home......probably used during the war, hopefully the last......*"

Greg gazed towards the building, dust now settling around the jagged opening.

"*Be prepared......there may be more...*"

Stepping inside, they paused. Splattered across the ground was a line of robots, some already in the corrosive process. At the far end of the room an illuminated board hung, mathematical diagrams drawn across it in yellow. Dangling wall charts covered every inch of vertical space.

There was a series of dark corridors, long and narrow. Down a selected passage they walked curiously, slowly, until they reached a metal door. Doug pushed and kicked at it, but it wouldn't open......Reaching for his laser-torch he burnt a neat circular hole, wide enough to pass through. Greg motioned him forward with his finger. Instantly, Doug stepped in, blast-gun in hand, Harris pressing behind....

"*It's clear Commander....*" Doug barked with relief... "*Nothing but large wooden boxes......some kind of cargo....*"

Greg stepped in, walking around the large dusty room. Across the ceiling, he noticed a long, broken half dangling wire. Underfoot, bits of broken glass crunched. Suddenly, three robots rushed into the room like insects, holding beam-rifles.

"*Freeze.....*" one rasped metallically.....

In a frenzy of panic, Doug and Harris fired, blowing the robots out of existence. All that remained were bits of metal, bundles of twisted metallic shell, wheels, bolts rolling into silence. Even sections of the walls had been penetrated, eaten away, gaping jagged holes billowing with smoke unveiling the outside world.

Doug bent down and twisted a beam-rifle from one of the robot's clenched humanoid hands. Standing up, he gazed at it, running his fingers over the smooth metal.

"*Interesting weapon.....*"

"*What do you think are in these boxes Commander?*" Harris asked, beating his fist against one, its rough wooden texture dust coated.

"*Whatever it is, feel free to take......remember we are authorised legally to bring back anything of use.....it was agreed by the galactic trade conference...signed and sealed before this mission....*"

Harris slid one open, placing the lid onto the ground. There was an odour of age and dust......

"*Minerals, metals, substances.....a whole selection from various planets in our solar system......Looks like whatever or whoever lived here were pirates...*" He shrugged stoically.

Greg moved over and peered inside... "*Pirates indeed.....don't you recognize these?*" He pointed. "*These mineral deposits and metals were stolen from us many years back during the galactic mining projects......a whole shipment....*"

"Oh yeah," Doug said reflectively.... "*There were several riots back home...it went down on the file as missing...nothing more...*"

"*That's right....without these....we would never have had temperature alternating buildings, even our advanced control equipment inside the rocket-ship depends on it in order to operate smoothly, effectively...*"

He placed his hand inside, gazing, touching.....turning.

"Bronomite," he smiled thinking back. "*That's what they use in customs back home, in order to get the truth from suspicious voyagers.....In dangerously high doses they can even use it to determine if a person is criminally minded and what types of crime he or she may plan in the future....it almost has a way of looking into future events, what may or may not happen, by detecting people's desires, plans, and tendencies......*"

He continued to explore inside the box......

"*Menzite......used in our vidscreens to create a 4-d effect.....Dolaphite used in medicine......helps fight against many forms of disease.....*"

He was caught in nostalgic thought....lamenting deeply.

"*They've even got hold of Kronian......the Kronian mines of Arcadon....*" He recalled the wars and riots there with the locals, distant but real images, scenes and sensations.

"*What's it used for?*" Doug inquired.

"*Aptitude testing apparatus....virtuosity....With it we can determine what occupation is best suited for us....measuring our intellect, and abilities. Kronian testers are used extensively all round, especially for recruiting Troopers....*"

Greg paused......then continued.

"*We have enough of these supplies to last us twenty generations and more....but that doesn't allow for pirates invading.....passing into prohibited zones unlawfully.*" He clenched his fist in anger.

"*When we get back, we'll determine whether or not it's worth mining here for natural resources......who knows what lies beneath us......*"

"*Hey, do you hear that Commander?*"

"*Hear what Doug?*"

"*That sound......wait.....listen!*"

Alerted, Harris nodded in disturbed agreement.

There was a ticking sound, constant but faint. An alarm rattled. They glanced at each other......

"*Quick let's get out of here,*" Greg commanded piercingly.

Rapidly working their way through the narrow corridor, they exited the building. At a set distance they dived for cover. In a flash the building exploded into a shapeless mass of rubble, smoke, fire and debris littering and lighting up the mid-afternoon sky. Greg turned back in horror, his dirt streaked view plate partially masking his sight. A spiralling dark cloud formed, unleashing toxic fumes into the already radioactive atmosphere.

"*That was close,*" Greg muttered with relief. "*Let's return to base.*"

The sun had set and the world was dark and still, creatures seeking refuge amongst the rubble and ash, a few stars glinting above escaping through the dense clouds of ash.

Outside the rocket-ship, Greg paced back and forth contemplating the day's events, his helmet-beam activated and bright. He flicked on his suit heater and continued, the helmet-beam cutting into the night darkness and lighting up a piece of jagged metal ahead of him. The scan-com suddenly flashed red, bleeping. Crouching on one knee, Harris lifted it from his belt, waving it into the air. Across the small screen, a spy ship was displayed, sleek, slender and aerodynamic. Rapidly, the ship descended, landing lights flickering on and off, brake jets igniting a fiery red.

As it touched down making contact with the surface of the planet, Harris reduced magnification, acquiring a multi-dimensional view of the surroundings, as well as the ship itself. He watched intently for motion and sound. Neither came.

"*Do you recognize it...one of ours?*"

"*No Commander.*" He turned the screen in his direction, enlarging the image of the ship. G-7 was marked across its slender frame.

"*Doug......prepare to fire....mark it down on the system as an illegal entry....don't forget....*"

"*Okay......*"

"*What are the coordinates at present?*"

Harris took a reading.

"*Eleven kilometres north-east......*"

"*Commander which gun do I activate, laser or vapour?*"

"*There's a strong night wind...considering the distance the vapour may lose its trajectory, and even then by the time the corrosive action takes place, they could escape...use laser...*"

In an instant, the ship lifted, spiralling into the atmosphere, its rapid movement causing the scan-com to lose track.

"*It's gone,*" Harris complained, the glare of the scan-com reflecting across the glass view plate of his helmet. "*It's as if they heard us....whatever they were...*"

It hovered for a time, stalking the skies, moving above a range of mountains and then disappeared into outer space, tearing through the planet's gravitational field at terrifying speed; severing the umbilical cord, gravity. The screen went blank. The red warning light deactivated, fading to green.

"*All clear Commander......*"

"*Good......lets get some rest......tomorrow we'll head out there...we need to investigate......*"

Greg stood alone for a time, gazing up into the sky as if for confirmation, the cold nocturnal stars now sliding in and out of a foggy mist. The planet was cooling off. Then he caught sight of an object, a meteor, soon to be burnt up in the atmosphere. '*Meteorological phenomenon,*' he thought. He turned, heading towards the ship.

The night was passing rapidly.....another day emerging, the dark fading into grey, the landscape slowly forming and taking shape in the growing light. Sunrise was beautiful, dimly masked by particles in suspension.

At the top of a hill, nine kilometres out from base, Greg could see the remains of a space-station, beyond it a city, gleaming white ruins scattered here and there.

"*Commander......*" Doug pointed indicating east. "*That's where the ship landed.....*"

Greg halted regaining breath, theorizing, thinking.

"*An old space-station......*"

He scanned its remains, a few buildings, others virtually demolished into a heap of metal and rubble. Cosmic-crafts were few, and those that remained we clearly inoperative, metal fatigue and structural damage clearly evident even from a distance.

"*Come, let's move on....*"

The space-station was now meters away. Beneath them lay an underground base, a semi-corroded metallic ladder leading to it below.

"*Doug......Harris, see what you can find. Report back here within twenty minutes...I'm going down....*"

As Greg descended, his boots clattered and echoed against the rusted metal of the ladder. Step by step he made his way down. Reaching the bottom, he stumbled backwards, promptly regaining equilibrium. His back ached.....a dull constant ache. The ground was wet, the underground base tubular in design. Robots lay motionless, broken in sections of decaying metal, beam-rifles and glass everywhere. There were rooms, generators, complex apparatus and wall charts of cosmic-crafts with listed destinations. Moving towards a dark room the beam from his helmet activated, cutting a white circular path in front of him. Across the ground he noticed sand and two long snaking wires. Squatting, he expertly traced them. They were connected into a black machine, clearly out of function. Then in thought, he picked up a handful of sand letting it trickle through his gloved fingers. After a few moments, he moved out.

Working his way back up, he reached the surface, the desolate landscape engulfing him through the mist and ash. Rain began to fall from the sky, drenching the alien planet in torrents of water. Turning a dial around on his belt, a small tube extended out from within the helmet, directing nutrition capsules into his mouth. He swallowed. Then from his tank, he pulled out an exhausted tube which carried the capsules, tossing it to the ground. Five remained, plenty to last him a week or more....the difference between life and death.

Cautiously he pushed on, debris crunching under him. Suddenly something metallic glittered. Most of it was concealed beneath the rubble and dirt.

Bending, he fought to retrieve it, gripping his hands around the exposed edge. Slowly he slid it out, and stood gazing at a large rusty telescope. A symbol was imprinted across it, nothing more. Then his transmitter bleeped into life. He blew against the mike......

"Commander...it's Harris......do you copy?" His voice came in distantly.

"Yes......I copy..."

A moment of wave interference......The rain increased, swirling with the wind......

"I just received telemetry with that craft, G-7.....the one we caught on the scan-com......They claim to be the only survivors from this planet." His voice began to fade, fading with breathless accomplishment.

"Planet Earth, Commander, that's the name they gave me....

The creatures describe themselves as humans......humans Commander......they call their new home Ganymede...one of Jupiter's moons......"

Greg clicked off the transmitter gazing above, smiling.... breathing in the controlled atmosphere. '*Earth*,' he muttered, '*humans, pirates. What other surprises lay ahead,*' he thought, '*in this semi-abandoned death planet?*'

Destination CITON

Stripping the winning lotto numbers from his weekly journal, Ed Rutherford dashed to the vid-phone with elated emotion. Instantly his mind lit up with images of new worlds, along with the reality that Earth would no longer be home....Speaking into the phone, he blasted out the three digit number and was immediately connected. After a few beeps, a voice spoke, a face forming on the vid-screen simultaneously.

"*Solar Voyages....*"

Caught in awe he moved his lips soundlessly....then composing himself replied almost stuttering... "*Yes, good morning....I've won, I have the winning numbers.*"

His green eyes sparkled, awaiting his prize. The invisible flame deep within him that had diminished over the years had suddenly reignited.

"*Identity code please*," the soft feminine voice chirped.

Across the palm of his left hand he read out the embedded code, "*ER-278....*"

Silently, briskly, the lady registered the data, her face on the vid-screen now concealed in waves of visual static.

"*Mr Ed Rutherford of 9, Olympia Drive, Los Angeles.....*"

"*Yes that's me*," he murmured excitedly, running his tongue around the edges of his mouth.

"*You can make your way over to head office.....the address is imprinted on the back of the winning digits.....*"

Guided by euphoric emotion he clicked off the vid-phone, swigged down a shot of warm whisky, and headed for the door.

At the L.A hover-station, he awaited his train impatiently oblivious to the world around him, his hands deep inside his coat pockets battling the chill. People, noise and restless chaos engulfed him, filling virtually every corner. A sudden wink of blue light from a forming hologram listing climatic data caught his attention; he was back, back in the world of reality. Then, his vc-watch buzzed. With idle concern, he lifted his wrist to his mouth covering the small screen with his hand, blocking out the visual portion of the transmission.

"*Hello.....*"

"*Ed where are you? You were supposed to be at work an hour ago......*"

"*Can't make it......talk later....got to go!*"

He deactivated the connection with the turn of a dial. He was in no mood for dialogue....especially with his boss, *'there was no need to interact with him anymore,'* he thought and then chuckled to himself. For a brief moment he pictured him, a tall lanky, bald, and intimidating figure of a man who vented his life's frustrations and deep insecurities on others, Ed just happened to be his favourite daily victim, it was nothing personal.

Moments later the hover-train arrived, its rusty metallic frame reflecting the bright overhead station lights. As the doors opened with a swish, a whole crowd of bodies hurtled into the opening, squeezing and pushing their way through, battling for the few remaining seats. Ed was able to remain calm; after all he had just won the greatest prize, a one way trip to a mystery paradise planet...a distant sphere faraway in another galaxy where life would be radically different....Only the mega rich and famous inhabited the other worlds. Most miserable humans just dreamt of the idea and longed for it in envy. *'A low paid vehicle salesman like me?'* he thought to himself, *'unlikely,'* but all that was about to change.

Walking up to a towering skyscraper within the confines of the densely populated city centre, a melting pot of cultures, Ed Rutherford pushed his way through the glass doors with ease. With a quick glance he located the reception area, where a chubby security guard sat half dazed with boredom, flicking through a creased news journal. He forced a smile, as Ed rushed over.

"*Good day, how can I help...?*"

"*I've come to make my claim...*"

"*Thirtieth floor Sir, brown door to your right......*"

As the express elevator came to a halt, Ed walked out heading towards a large brown door where a bright glowing sign captured his attention, *'Solar Voyages.'* Adjusting his sandy blond hair, he was about to press the buzzer, but before he could move, the door slid open. Standing before him was a dynamic looking man, in his thirties wearing a distinctive green bow tie.

"*Clark O'Bryan.....You are?*"

He extended his slender hand in greeting.....they shook, then a moment of hesitation.

"*Ed Rutherford.*" A smile began to spread across his face.

"*Please Mr Rutherford come this way.*"

After a brisk walk down a long corridor filled with sound and activity, he was led into a large office. Barely containing his emotion, Ed placed the strip of winning lotto numbers on a desk then sat in a grey swivel chair, biting at the edges of his mouth in expectancy. Across the wall a vid-com suddenly flashed, a red and green light which constantly alternated, followed by a ping and then another.

"*Excuse me,*" Mr O'Bryan said, strolling over to the vid-com. "*Yes...*" There was a rapid exchange of words, no more than a few seconds....the call terminating quickly. Then, he took the luminous strip of winning digits, gazed at them for a time and started to walk purposefully to the back of the office towards a D-UNIT; a compact piece of machinery that extended from the floor midway to the ceiling. Standing before it, he punched in the numbers with deliberation. Ed's faced formed on the screen digitally in a three dimensional format. Having completed its mobile phases the machine shut down, now visually inoperative. There was a brief pause......with a sharp turn he walked over towards Ed smiling.

"*Congratulations Sir, you are the luckiest man alive and that's not just a figure of speech....from the records I see that this was your very first entry.....and consequently you won straight off....it almost defies the laws of probability....We have one annual winner.....you Sir, are lucky number five......*"

Ed leapt up gripping the man's hand. It suddenly dawned on him just how fortunate he was. He had only entered the lotto once, a few days back, a spontaneous half-hearted decision......and now he found himself the winner.

"*Thanks...I....I can't believe it myself. When do I leave?*"

"*First things first, Mr Rutherford......please, sit down.*"

He fell back into the swivel chair, wheeling himself over towards the front of the desk.

"*I'm sure you're longing to know where your awaited destination is.....*"

With his eyes Ed urged him on, moistening his lips......

"*But before I satisfy your curiosity, I need to clarify one little factor...*"

There was a brief silence......

"*You must understand Mr Rutherford, that under no circumstances can anyone join you...it's for you alone. This applies irrevocably to all, unless married.*"

For a loner like Ed the news wasn't going to cause any waves or turbulent feelings, after all, he had only himself to worry about, no friends, no family, only associates......it was ideal.

"Shall we continue?"

Ed nodded in agreement, locking his hands and cracking his knuckles.

"The planet is Citon. Galaxy Andromeda, 2.2 million-light years away....the nearest neighbouring large galaxy......"

"I knew......I knew it...." Ed blurted out.

"Tell me, is it really that beautiful......?"

Mr O'Bryan's eyes lit with assurance. *"Yes of course Sir, it's the place where dreams are made of,"* he uttered articulately. *"Of all the planets Citon is very special...you're a fortunate man......"*

Adjusting his bow tie with conviction, he sat down and then continued explaining......

"The landscape of this marvellous planet is diverse, to say the least. There are mountains, lakes, rivers, endless verdant fields which stretch as far as the eye can see......not to mention a wide variety of animal life......"

"Go on," Ed said with excitement.

"There are two suns perpetually shining......two giant heat radiating orbs. In the evening the temperature lowers radically, but it's certainly no colder than here. There is also an incredible variety of plant life found nowhere else in the galaxy......"

Sweat broke out across Ed's forehead. He could barely contain himself as his mind began building images around the words uttered.

"And......and, a house....?"

"You will be living in a mansion.....exactly one mile from the nearest centre where there are shops, restaurants, bars and all the other evening entertainment spots which will fulfil your day and nocturnal desires with unlimited credits to spend......"

Ed smiled, absorbing the information, greedily assimilating the facts.

"Now with regard to the departure date...how soon do you want to leave? It's totally your choice......"

Ed's expression signalled his intent.

"I'll leave tomorrow......"

"Great.....at the spaceport you'll meet one of our reps.....it's a formality with all our winners......"

In the idle hours of daylight, and before his bed alarm could ring, something inside prodded him, an inner remote reflex....his trip...the numbers. He awoke, slowly opening his eyes and assembling his scattered thoughts cohesively. In swift motion he slipped out of bed and stretched. The image of Citon flashed in his mind dissolving his morning drowsiness, accompanied by a smile. It wouldn't be long now before he saw the alien world in all its beauty and splendour. Raising his arm he checked the time as the morning sunlight shone across his face.

Then leaning over towards the vid-phone by the side of his bed, he dialled for a hover-cab. Arrival time was displayed across the screen almost instantly; twenty minutes was all he had. In a quick and coordinated burst of activity, he dashed towards his cupboard and began changing. Of course there wasn't the need to pack, he was about to commence a whole new fresh chapter in his life. *'The bed,'* he thought, *'clothes, house, it could all go to that half crazed Landlord.....it was more than adequate to make up the three months arrears......'*

Within no time he was airborne, inside the hover-cab, flying above the skyscrapers of downtown LA, blending in with the endless tide of air-vehicles. Below he could vaguely distinguish human life, as the faint images of people and surface-vehicles moved around in a circuitry of motion. *'Earthly existence,'* he muttered to himself, *'what a pain and struggle, but not anymore....'*

The hover-cab began a gliding descent; the world was approaching fast. Having descended onto terra aided by anti-gravity technology, he paid the driver by swiping his hand before the credit-reader and then stepped out, gazing at the huge sun shimmering spaceport which stood before him. Then from seemingly nowhere, a crew of reporters circled around him. Before he had time to digest the scene, a trans-cord device was shoved up to his gaping mouth. He took a step back, wondering, watching....listening.

"Sir, please tell our global-viewers how it feels to be this year's lucky lotto winner......"

The crew drew closer, a few tourists turned and muttered to each other in awe and admiration. Ed was gripped with a sense of pride and achievement. A mere chance in a billion, picking those seven winning digits had leapt him into stardom....the game of chance had paid off. Standing there in reflected glory he tried to compose himself, battling to find the correct words to match his star-like image. All eyes focused on him. He gesticulated and then spoke into the device.

"*There are no words to describe it...none....*" he said with an almost iconic tone.

"*Is it true that you only entered the lotto once.....and consequently won it straight off?*"

"*Yes indeed......I can't believe it myself......really...that's all I have to say.....*"

With flushed cheeks he edged his way through the crew of reporters and headed directly for the entrance of the spaceport. Having entered, a female rep from Solar Voyages walked over to Ed seductively. Her voluptuous body, jet black hair and crystal blue eyes drew great attention....

"*Mr Rutherford, I'm Marianne Lee, I trust you are all set to go?*"

"*Yes*", he answered, his eyes straying away timidly, gazing at a large travel-screen which displayed its usual holiday package deals. He refocused.

"*Please Sir, follow me......*"

He followed without replying, his eyes and mind elsewhere. Walking past the converging crowds he was led to a doorway. Security guards stood either side, dressed in their familiar pale blue uniforms.

"*Congratulations Sir,*" one to the left muttered tipping his cap.

Ed grinned and with a nod of his head accepted the guard's kind words. As doors slid apart, they stepped in, a row of yellowish light marking the way down. Cold air circled around them. His heartbeat began to increase. At the far end of the hall sat the latest transportation mechanism, which only the mega rich and government agents could afford, a revolutionary teleport operating homeostatically, without human attention. It sat there, luminous and inviting, and appeared to absorb light rather than reflect it.

Gazing at it, Ed began to feel a sense of fear which temporarily gripped him inwardly. Pointing over he said, "*I've heard all about this new machine, but how reliable is it?*"

The woman smiled, registering his concerns.....

"*Sir, people spend millions of credits on this daily, you can be sure that it is the most reliable transportation mechanism in the world, however, it's not unusual to feel a touch nervous, especially if it's your first time. It's the only way you can travel to other galaxies with instantaneous effect. Come let me explain."*

They walked over to it and then halted, Ed recapturing some of his lost composure.

"Within a matter of seconds you will find yourself on Citon, at the spaceport. The process is simple...you will be disassembled and then reassembled very quickly. As I'm sure you are well aware, we are a cluster of atoms, particles. This device breaks up the atomic structure, in this case yours, storing it, and then reassembling it in mathematical order, at the set destination....However, to explain how you are propelled through the universe would take me a life time...."

Ed stood there impressed by her rapid explanation. Although completely lost, he appeared to grasp the general idea.

"Are you ready Mr Rutherford?" she said soothingly.

He nodded, although his expression suggested the reverse. Walking over into a circle of flickering lights, he stood, now calm and cool. Around him the machine came into life, as if it were a living entity of its own. With the click of a switch, the lady released a lever which in turn caused a humming sound, a flow of energy. Above Ed's head, a fiery beam of white light fell, consuming him into nothingness......In a flash his image reappeared, materialising into existence. Opening his eyes he found himself standing before a young man. From his attire alone, Ed knew he was in another world. The man lowered his hat in greeting, yet something in his keen glance troubled Ed.

"Welcome to Citon, I'm your host, Jasper......" He smiled.

Ed returned the seemingly fabricated smile. Gazing around at the well-lit hallway, he could almost sense the alien world that lay beyond the confines of the spaceport. It reminded him that he was light years from Earth......

"Mr Rutherford, shall we commence our journey to your home..?

"Yes," he replied. Without further dialogue, the man turned and started to walk slowly towards the end of the long hall, Ed pressing close behind. As they approached the door it appeared to melt away, once through, it reformed quickly. Striding through a semi-empty spaceport they came to the exit, where a neon sign flashed in red, *'Welcome to Citon.'* For a brief moment, the whole experience felt remarkably familiar. Somewhere in the back of his mind it echoed, he could almost recall it

vividly, but how, perhaps somewhere in his dreams? With a shrug of his shoulders, he dismissed the subject without further probing.

Exiting the spaceport, he gazed into the hazy mid-afternoon alien sky. It was captivating and brilliant. Suspended in the distance, like two giant eyes were the suns diffusing an unearthly light, and the land for miles appeared to shimmer and glow majestically. All of a sudden, something alive staggered over his thumb, an alien life form, tiny and yellow, ant-like. Intrigued by it, he watched its movements as it amazingly appeared to mutate and alter its colour.

Brushing it from his thumb, the insect fell, disappearing into the dry grey soil below. That moment proved decisive. It catapulted him from his child-like approach to one more serious and questioning; the psychological transition was instant. What a sudden twist of fate! His whole life had swung from one of emptiness to this, all hinged on one spontaneous decision, one which had paid off handsomely. But what was it that motivated him to enter the lotto? How was it possible to win straight off? He probed his mind in search of logical answers to the bizarre sequence of events and improbabilities that led to his present success....none enlightened him, it was futile, yet he savoured the moment, taking in his first deep breath of alien air....this was now home......

Walking over to an air-vehicle, the host pulled out a small sensitive control gadget from his pocket, and began manipulating it. The doors of the vehicle opened slanting upwards and its anti-gravity operating mechanism came into life. Steadily and maintaining equilibrium, they ascended into the sky, hovering above the planet's equator. Leaning over to one side Ed admired the beauty down below. The bird's eye view was spectacular, almost an earth like environment, filled with lakes and rivers like liquid silver, an ocean, mountains, endless green fields......yet the peculiar haze in the atmosphere and the two scorching suns conspired to remind him that he was indeed in another galaxy......

Reaching the ground, the air-vehicle came to a halt. Guided by curiosity, Ed quickly slid the door open and stepped out onto the stony ground. From the soles of his shoes he could feel vibrations that signified life and activity. Then he noticed that directly in front of him, stood a mansion which had an almost liquid crystal colour......a peculiar grey with a network of leaves and branches covering a small section of it. Surrounding it in all directions were beautiful fields abounding with colourful plants the likes of which he had never seen, broken occasionally by tall white gleaming buildings, some pyramid shaped, others vertical and narrow. Turning his head towards his host, he raised his hand and pointed at the mansion.

"That's mine?"

"Yes Mr Rutherford, that's yours," the man replied.

Ed was captivated by its elaborate design, the whole scene had somewhat numbed him of emotion. Fresh energy stirred within him. Waving his hand before the code beam, the plush white doors slid apart, retracting into the walls for concealment. Ed stepped in, his host following behind.

"So Mr Rutherford, is it to your liking?"

With a sharp turn he replied. *"To my liking..? Yes....yes it is...."*

His voice trailed off, his mind now engaged in deep thought. Again a wave of fascinated awe swept through him. That feeling of familiarity gripped him, pestering his mind. Even the air had a nostalgic scent to it, but he still couldn't quite pinpoint nor equate what it was. With his eyes he scanned the surroundings, the light pink sofa, the vision-screen, the stone floor; everything was pleasing and inviting.

"Well, Mr Rutherford," his host exclaimed, *"I'll leave you to it."* From his pocket, he pulled out a complex looking device, placing it into Ed's palm.

"Here, if you need anything you can dial a hologram from this."

Tipping his hat politely he left, the doors sliding back into place, cutting off the faint sounds and muffled echoes from outside. Alone and tired Ed paced about. Through a curtained window he caught a glimpse of the town, distant shapes of people and life. He could vaguely distinguish a line of tall hard structures, but the bright haze concealed most of it. Striding towards the kitchen he paused at the entrance, dutifully activating the device. Immediately a hologram appeared, taking on the form of a young man....

"Welcome Mr Rutherford, please make your requests known..."

Ed laughed. *'Interesting toy,'* he thought, tossing it into the air and catching it. Everything was perfect, almost too perfect. With the turn of a dial the hologram faded, blurring and twisting into an oscillating haze and then nothingness. Placing the device down onto the translucent kitchen-table, he strolled back into the lounge, where he sat sinking into the sofa. He sighed. He felt tired, yet mentally lucid.

Then, midway to the ceiling, he spotted something he hadn't initially noticed. He scratched his head curiously gazing up at a machine that sparked into life. It discharged an array of sounds like rebounding radar signals at an unusual frequency, and then began to descend towards him slowly, guided and manipulated by mechanical arms. He adjusted himself, sitting rigid as the machine halted before him. It became apparent it was some sort of vision-set, silver and bulky, unlike the one in the corner of the room. The screen came alive and a computer animated face formed. Through an audio system current passed from transformer to speaker, and a mechanical voice suddenly droned, "*Sebastian.....*"

Ed sat back baffled, anxious eyes igniting with wonder. Although the name was clearly unknown to him, it seemed to have a strange kind of significance. Again from the screen the voice spoke, "*Sebastian......*"

"*Who are you?*" Ed demanded nervously.

"*There is a technical error....your time here has now expired...*"

"*What! What are you talking about?*" He paused. 'This is ridiculous,' Ed thought, '*I've only just arrived.*' Before he could think any further, the image replied......

"*Actually you have been here quite sometime.*"

"*Wait a minute, I never spoke.*"

"*Indeed you didn't.*"

"*Hey what kind of game is this?*" Ed shouted, defiant in his attitude....his anxiety perpetuating.

The screen grew brighter, the animated image with it, yet the man's features were still indistinguishable. Ed began to realise something was desperately wrong. '*Machines couldn't read people's thoughts, could they?*' Moving towards the machine in fascination, he began to touch and prod his way around in search of answers, his face working spasmodically.

"*Sebastian......*"

He leapt back mystified and replied, pointing at the screen.

"*Why do you keep calling that, I'm Ed?*"

There was no immediate reply, only silence met the convoluted echoes of his mind. An interval passed in which the machine appeared inoperative. Taking in a breath of air, Ed began to regain a measure of calm, almost as if he was resigning himself to the fact that a sinister reality awaited. His eyes were focused, fixed on the screen......

"*I'm afraid to inform you that due to a technical malfunction, you are not Ed Rutherford,*" the image said suddenly, now slightly higher pitched.

Ed laughed, but there were ripples of fear and tension in his voice.

"*So who am I then?*"

"*You are Sebastian Eckardt, an interplanetary Spy......*"

"*Really,*" Ed replied sarcastically..... "*Sure....*"

"*You see Sebastian, everything that you see and feel is fabricated...a virtual world......you yourself decided to have the virtual journey implanted in your head in order to escape the reality of your incarceration on Citon....that implantation proved unsuccessful.*"

"*What implantation?*" he yelled out abruptly.....

"*The one that you requested......*"

"*Are you telling me that I'm living in a simulated world, and that nothing around me is real....including myself?*" He banged his fist against the arm of the sofa to emphasize his point.

"*Precisely,*" the screen flashed with its reply.

"*So, if that's the case, you're not real either?*"

"*Incorrect, I'm very real, a highly advanced program inside your head guiding you out of fantasy into reality...*"

Ed was gripped by that odd familiar feeling, the one which had haunted him since his arrival. He was totally immobile in thought...

"*You see Sebastian, after your sentence three months ago down on Earth, you were sent here with two options. The options were as follows: To live out the remainder of your life on this abandoned hazardous planet Citon with hundreds of other criminals until death, facing the daily deadly realities around you. The second option was to live on the hazardous planet, strapped to a highly advanced machine where you would live out a virtual trip of your choice, the very one implanted in your head where you took on a whole new identity, a humane approach and option to your crime......In your case you chose Ed Rutherford, the low paid vehicle salesman who had just won the lotto...and was about to embark on a new life on the paradise planet Citon......But the truth is Citon is nothing more than a death planet, far from what the virtual trip is portraying......*"

"*Wait a minute,*" Ed said leaping to his feet, "*let's get this straight......How do you explain all my memories since childhood, are they all virtual too?*"

"*They are nothing more than false implants, an artificial construct. During the implantation your true memory bank was erased, with it your identity. All past events, every single memory and emotion you experienced as Ed Rutherford are false....*"

Ed fell back into his seat, caught in a web of confusion and terrifying doubt, yet he fought down his feelings and thoughts....it all felt too real, everything so tangible, even the mundane scent of his body was too real to question. Then regaining his composure, he spoke out to the machine.....

"*So why now......why have you chosen to reveal this to me if I'm really in a virtual world....and how long have I been like this...?*

Again the computerized voice replied, "*You were set to live out your life in this delusionary world of Ed Rutherford until death by laser-vaporization, which is instant, had it not been due to a technical malfunction....I am programmed to reveal all to you in the unfortunate event...as it is proving....With regards to the time period, you have been in this virtual world two months...*"

"*That can't be...*"

"*It is futile to compare time lapses between reality and fantasy.....there is no sense of chronology attached.....*"

The voice now became slow, muffled, distant and metallic...

"*Soon you will awaken from this virtual world and see for the very first time......*"

Suddenly, there was a sound, a ticking sound which appeared to come from out of nowhere. The sound grew louder, almost deafening. Covering his ears with his hands, Ed was gripped in immobilizing fear. Then, from the machine, a beam of light followed in a wave, passing above Ed's head, fading moments later. The most complex part of its cycle now came, as the program reached its final phase of operation.

"*What's happening to me?*" Ed yelled......

At that precise moment, as if deactivated, sunlight was no more. He looked up with a startled gaze. All he could see were objects twisting and fading, expanding and retracting then collapsing into a vacuum of space and obscurity. Everything that surrounded him was obliterated by this deepening blackness which swirled around, yet oddly the animated figure across the screen remained intact, brighter and more real than before. Reaching out he tried to touch it, the only seemingly tangible object that now remained in his universe, but that too soon faded into a shapeless mass of non-existence. Then darkness, total darkness......

Suddenly he awoke, his blurred eyes registering with reality. Torn with confusion he instinctively pulled a mask from his face which was connected via a trailing wire to a black bulky machine. It was functioning at maximum capacity, monitoring his respiration and heart rate via stethoscopic sensors, registering his body temperature which was then displayed across a screen in luminous green digits. Still it functioned, recording and depositing neuro-chemical activity within its database, operating in synchronicity. Then, it deactivated. Although inoperative, it continued to oscillate in lateral motion.

With a shaky hand he wiped his gaunt face, which was drenched in hot sticky sweat. His eyes were dark with exhaustion. He took a deep breath fighting to take in the thin weak air and then exhaled in convulsive relief.

On his left arm he noticed a syringe inserted into his bicep. Connected to it, was a dangling long tube which trailed off towards yet another machine. Through the tube, a yellowish fluid passed......a complex food source. Vigorously he pulled at it until it loosened, tossing it away. As the syringe hit the floor it cracked open, the yellowish fluid leaking out. Slowly, the fluid began to solidify and transform into a dense gooey substance as it met with the atmosphere......

Gazing around, he noticed a corroded metallic door. Struggling to his feet, he began to make his way for the exit. For the first time he realised that he was in some kind of spherical shaped chamber. Barely maintaining his balance, he staggered to the door pushing it apprehensively. It swung open with a creak. Instantly, powerful blinding sunlight struck him. He immediately raised his hands in an attempt to shield his eyes from the sun. Warily he stepped out and gazed into the horizon, barely distinguishing the other chambers in the distance. They were glowing, shining silver and metallic in the alien light.

Sebastian stood there motionless, with no recollection of his past, his mind void and empty, the memory of his trip now fading away into a meaningless blur...... Dust swirled around him blown by a gust of wind, his eyes reflecting the huge shimmering orb of the sun. Ahead the land stretched for miles without moisture of any kind. An endless arid wilderness of scorching sun and broken rock engulfed him. Death was certain...he stood at its mercy, at the mercy of the unforgiving world......Citon!

Spy Hunter

A blade-roller halted beside the waiting line at the business end of level 4. Reece stepped towards it, past the angry line of five, holding out his card. The passenger door ejected open.

"*Spy Hunter, hey....where to?*" the cab driver asked cordially...

Reece slid in, leaning back in relaxed mode.

"*Level 1 please....*"

The driver shook his head with esteem.

"*Don't get too many Hunters nowadays......*"

The blade-roller was now in motion, disappearing through the endless underground network of tubular metallic passages.....

Stretched across the continent of America, a subterranean human existence dwells. The remainder of the planet is lifeless....only a selected few venture to the surface...specially licensed killers known as Spy Hunters. After the war, three centuries back, Earth was left in ruin. Hard radiation had caused mutations at all levels. Only a few tribal mutants roamed the surface of the planet in search of food, fighting for survival amongst death and destruction......but another unknown creature stalked the surface.....with deadly intentions.....

Working its way up through the various levels, the roller halted smoothly at L1. The footpath was bare, no sound or motion. Overhead, an oxygen system droned, powerful jets blasting out cold re-purified air....

"*Always empty up here......boring if you ask me......*"

Reece smiled in acknowledgement, his dark brown eyes full of expression.

"*What do I owe?*"

"*Twenty please.....*"

He stretched out his hand and laid it against the credit collector. Briskly it registered and bleeped. A white glow of light seeped through his fingers and around the edges of his hand....

"*Credit stored,*" a recorded female voice chimed softly.

The door slid open.

"*Must be a fascinating occupation,*" the driver said half grinning with admiration. "*Tell me.....what's it like on the surface....?*"

Reece halted, one foot outside on the firm ground.

"*A dead, silent, radioactive world.....at dawn a burning sun, at nightfall a cold moon lighting the evening sky...*"

The driver interjected.

"I hope I live long enough to see it, to see the rhythm of the day and night, even one small miserable glance. Do you think we will ever reclaim the surface, revive earth again....I mean grow food in the ground as our ancestors once did......?"

"Maybe one day......Thanks for the ride...."

Stepping out, the blade-roller began to move, disappearing down the tube, southbound towards the commercial centre. Reece raised his jacket collar and commenced his walk towards the GDS assembly point, a short distance off. Consulting his wristwatch, he realised twenty minutes remained before his meeting with Lawrence Parker, head of the Government Defence system; another mission, a deadly assignment. Moments later he was there. Outside in glowing lights were the words *'Defenders of the Planet.'*

Waving his hand in front of the code beam, he pushed through the heavy revolving doors, and entered.

"Hi Reece," the secretary said in her usual flirtatious fashion, her eyes crystal green, her aging body well preserved by hormones and specialised rejuvenation processes. He shot her a warm glance, immediately disengaging his focus as he walked into the meeting room. As always, the room was meticulously arranged, rows of chairs and desks systematically positioned. A large monitor screen hung against the wall, seemingly in suspension.

"Hey..." Casper grumbled, half way across the room, lowering his paper, his nails cracked and broken......his face lined with fatigue, short blond hair wet and spiked. *"On time......"*

Reece was momentarily startled. He moved over, dropping into the chair beside him.

"I didn't see you......caught me off guard...."

"Sorry buddy......Did you hear?" His voice became hard, serious. *"It's just the two of us...."*

"I knew it....office gossip, never accurate. I was told it was three, me you and Wilson...."

"Not anymore Reece......Why they keep cutting down in numbers for such dangerous missions is beyond me....anything to save a few bucks......"

Reece lay back listening, cool and composed; a vital characteristic in such a deadly nerve wracking job.

"I guess they can't help picking the best, strategic reasons." He winked and smiled, nudging him with a sharp elbow......

Suddenly Lawrence Parker walked in, shutting the door behind him. He was a short stocky man, partially bald with bowed legs, his gold coloured uniform glinting in the light. He smiled across at them thinly, an unlit cigar jammed in his mouth.

"Good day gentlemen......"

"How's it going Parker?" Reece inquired.

"That depends......"

Parker regulated the lights from a remote control, dimming the room into virtual darkness. Instantly the monitor screen lit up; a white, blank shimmering square of light. Parker walked over and halted beside the screen, Reece and Casper focused on him, alert and attentive.

"Let's make this short and get down to business...."

He paused, lighting his cigar. At last he spoke.

"We have brief footage of a creature stalking the surface....one we do not recognize, anatomically different from the others in terms of its physical appearance."

"How many are there?" Casper exclaimed, his voice clipped and intense.

"The surface field detector suggested the presence of around four to five......"

There was an interval of silence as he puffed away, the cigar glowing red.

"What are they, who sent them....?" Reece asked, ideas flashing, twisting through his mind. *'The outspacers...the battles.....the past missions....'*

"Can't be certain...if you want a conjectural analysis....perhaps skin covered robots...perhaps totally biological...man-made of course...in answer to the other question.....they could be from anywhere....we have many enemies scattered throughout the galaxy and beyond......"

"Can they replicate?"

"Replication......methods of replication, who knows Reece, that's a good question. If they are biological they probably can....."

Casper gazed over at Reece apprehensively, eyes widening.

"We don't even know what we're facing...."

Parker continued, breaking the flow of their whispered conversation.

"We need to move fast, it's vital.....no time to waste...it's already been two days since the alarm...we can't afford to hesitate. I would hate to think what would happen down here if they gained access......"

"R-BOMBS......*kamikazes*," Casper rasped...

"*Yes, those are my suspicions. Most of our enemies deploy the same tactics, get under and destroy, whether using robots or biologically made creatures to fulfil the task......*"

"*Hey man,*"....Reece muttered under his breath, tugging Casper by the arm......"*Those bombs set off a series of deadly controlled explosions which move for miles.....we will have to be extra cautious with our approach......we can't use blaster guns....only rays...*"

"*No question about it......The worst is, R-Bombs are virtually untraceable.....especially when the carrier has them internally implanted......scanners are unreliable....*"

"*Here, take a look at these images captured last night....*" Parker said pointing at the monitor. He manipulated the remote control and the blank screen changed, displaying the dead night surface of earth.

The cold moon was visible through the swirling mists, the jagged mountains fading into the darkness and night vapours. He sped up the scenes into a blur of energy. Seconds later he slowed it down. A creature now came into view moving in jerky swift strides, lurking in the shadows. He spun a dial blowing up the figure until it was fully distinguishable. Pressing the pause button, he captured the moment....The man-made creature was completely biological, slightly bent and hairless, its physiology mimicking that of a human, two legs, two arms, hands, feet, slender frame, except that its skull was elongated, with big slanting multi-lensed eyes, a tiny slit for a mouth and no visible nose or ears.

"*What an ugly creature....*" Casper said sharply in revulsion, tapping his mechanical pencil against his lip repetitively.

Lawrence released the pause button, shutting down the monitor. Instantly light was restored around the room. Reece blinked, adjusting to it.

"*So guys, by eight am tomorrow report here...I'm aiming to get you out on the surface by ten.....*"

Casper rubbed his jaw in thought, his tough bristles spiking into his skin.

"*In terms of their capabilities, characteristics, we don't have all the info...we haven't been able to monitor their movements that much. From your point of exit at location A, you should detect them within a ten mile radius.......At this stage I can't be certain of anything......"*

Back at his apartment Reece sat, vodka in hand chilled with a cube of ice. In the corner the tele-set was live and active, faintly audible; the sole news channel playing. After a time of reflection, he had finally pieced together and absorbed all the information from his meeting with Parker.

From the adjoining kitchenette, Christina walked over, passing from a zone of bright light into the recessed lighting of the living room. She sat beside him, arranging herself gracefully, her silk robe falling across the floor, hazel eyes warm and immense. Around her neck, a chain of colourful gems rested. He shifted his gaze towards her......

"Reece......you ok......?"

"Yeah babe......" he replied unconvincingly.

"Don't you think it's about time you took a break? You deserve a well earned rest......"

"Maybe one of these days......"

Her expression became serious.

"I know it pays well....but I wish you'd find another post within the GDS......seventeen years is a long time......it's not like you are the only one, they've got up to forty registered Hunters..."

She broke off, almost inviting him to agree.

"I mean an enormous corporation like this...."

"Christina......by law a Spy Hunter retires at 45, it's mandatory, that gives me another ten years before I can even contemplate a managerial post......"

Her eyes, which were fixed on him, did not waver, vague emotions stirring within her. She stroked his face.

"Oh well," he said shrugging his shoulders. He knocked back his drink, the ice cube falling into his mouth and melting promptly into liquid.

"How long will you be gone for......?"

He chose his words carefully; the risk factor was high.

"Can't say......It may prove to be a long tedious process, but hopefully not...."

She pressed her hand against his chest.

"Please be careful......"

"I will......as always......"

From his pocket he yanked out a ticket...

"Here...." he said holding onto her arm gently....his tender grip affirming his love and concern......

"*What's this?*"

"*A ticket to sector 1......*"

She pondered for a time, visibly surprised.

"*That's below the old state of California.....*"

"*Correct....The blade-roller will get you there within four hours.....*"

"*But why......?*"

"*Sector 4 has been under constant attack....whilst I'm away I want you out of here, somewhere safe.....it's getting real dangerous....if an R-Bomb kamikaze carrier gets under.....*"

He paused....eyes cold and distant...

"*Trust me....for some reason our sector is the main target at present.....you are in much danger....*"

"*But....but, I thought the critical period was over......Why these stupid news reporters and daily broadcasts have us believing it's just propaganda, I will never know......*"

"*Christina they have to......if everyone knew the truth they would leave....sector 4 would be empty......and the other sectors would be flooded with an overload of worried people....*"

"*Okay......*" she said resigning to the fact, the same classical resignation he had seen countless times before. "*I'll go pack a bag......get some bits together....*"

The next morning Reece and Casper sat in the launching chamber. Above was the exit, two thick metallic doors which separated the underground world with the surface. Gazing up Reece could sense the desolation, the remoteness that awaited them, with it the danger. Dressed in their atmospheric suits, their masks were secured, protecting them against the eye damaging sunlight that was to come. Automatically, the mask-filtering-system activated; a refined mechanism that blocked out the hazardous airborne particles that hovered above Terra, allowing in clean oxygen. Attached to their belts were blasters, ray-guns, scanners, and small tracking devices that detected distant energy fields. Reece raised his thumb.

"*Let's do it.....*"

From the mask-fitted transmitter, he gave the command...

"*Duke......we're all set...*"

"*Did you take the nutrition-hydro capsule....? You may well be out there for a number of days.....*"

"*Yes.....*"

"*Okay, keep us informed of your progress.....and good luck....*"

"*Thanks......*"

The echoes from his last words faded with a series of crackles, as the transmitter deactivated. The metal ground beneath them began to move with a hum, lifting steadily, elevating like a mini platform towards the now parting metallic doors. Sunlight and a blue sky soon became visible, light seeping through with an alien-like effect. A cold shiver rushed through them, suppressed by rigid determination to see out the task. As they reached the surface they moved onto the arid ground. It resembled a wilderness, hot and dry, desolation and silence everywhere, but for the faint cries of hovering birds that came and went every now and then.

Far off, jagged mountains were visible, vivid, framed in the brilliant light. A lizard like creature suddenly moved across the ground in search of refuge. It disappeared amongst piles of brick and steel, the remains of a city, hard tall structures that once stood and graced the land; relics of the past. The platform now began to descend, the doors shutting simultaneously.

"*Welcome to Nevada with its sunlight. The diurnal nocturnal circle again.*" Casper cut off emphatically.

Manipulating the tracking device, Reece captured the presence of life, stretching over three miles to the north.

"*Casper, look....*" He squeezed his arm. "*Cephalic activity...*"

Across the luminous screen, a red light pulsed in varied sections of the map showing areas of movement, a detailed network of green lines and squares.

"*It could well be mutant colonies....they are scattered all over.....the furthest point of activity is 3.2 miles away.....after that, nothing......*"

"*Yeah, well I guess we should make headway,*" Casper replied....eyeing him with cold bright eyes......

"*The good thing is.....the device has picked up energy fields around the same congregated area. Just one straight path north.....it's easy enough.*"

Reece pointed back at the screen, towards a section that displayed climatic data.

"The planet seems to be cooling off, who knows what the future brings.....perhaps the surface can be reclaimed.....one day......"

Trudging over the rugged landscape, the poisonous wind lashed around them, twisting across the ruined surface of earth, its sound a roar reminiscent of a past existence. Heaps of rubble and remnants of civilization lay scattered across the barren hostile land, rotting......rusting, metal bent and twisted. Lifeless trees swayed back and forth, sapped dry of their moisture, shrivelling in the heat. Above, the sun shone like a blinding orb of fire; there was no escape from its clutches.

Occasionally they passed the odd mutant community, tiny huts made out of timber and scrap metal, tribe after tribe of small silent communities that gazed over at them in awe, like lost children in search of guidance....hope. Groups sat around like primitives, huddled together in rags and animal skins, conversing, jesting, others cleaning weapons, knives, arms rising and falling, gesticulating, chattering murmurs of voices drifting back and forth, an inconceivable spectacle of barbaric existence. Most were short but well built. The whites of their eyes appeared to shine, contrasting against their black leathery skin that was dirt stained, ravaged with hot burning sweat and fatigue.

"Damn mutants......freaks," Casper snapped irritably.... *"It's as if they are at another evolutionary stage....a bit like Neanderthal man...."*

"I don't believe in that evolutionary theory....."

"Opinion Reece.....however, it's amazing how their bodies have adapted to withstand such a hostile atmosphere and terrain, toxic winds, air....good survival instincts I guess......"

Reece nodded in agreement, and replied.

"They're certainly not sterile that's for sure......they've increased in number......It's the most I've seen at any one time.....but don't forget they are Homo-Sapiens just like us.....perhaps to them we are the mutants......"

"Come on, look at them. They're hideous......"

Reece butted in sharply......

"The war....the hydrogen explosions thinned the atmosphere, don't forget......the sun is unforgiving, merciless. I guess that's why there's such a startling contrast. Under the surface there is no ultraviolet light to raise the pigment level, nothing to burn the

skin...react with the melanin, that's why subterranean humanity has evolved differently and consequently lost skin colour. It's an environmental issue, food intake and so forth, nothing more. It doesn't make this gene-damaged society inferior......"

Casper consulted his tracking device, his thoughts and attention straying to it......

"Just one more section of red......a mile to go......once we've passed those ruins we'll be close.....let's keep going.....momentum at a time like this is vital."

Reece gave the thumbs up, and they moved, disappearing between the ruins at increasing pace. Within a short time they were a hundred metres away from their target. Ahead they could see a huge space-ship. It lay across the hostile bleak ground at a tilt, unbalanced by the uneven rocky landscape. It was silver and smooth, nothing complex looking, spherical in shape. Evidently occupied.

Reece moved forward concealing himself behind a huge rock, Casper near by. Beneath them lay a small patch of dry yellowish green grass; dead wispy strands.

"Okay....that's got to be them...."

Casper squatted, breaking the gravity effect which alleviated the built up strain on his legs. An oppressive fatigue had now set in, almost draining, immobilising his body. He gazed at the ship with intense curiosity, concealed from view in the dark shadow of the rock..."*It doesn't resemble any we've seen before......a first class ship.....*"

"I know.....Remember we can't use blasters......if they are R-Bomb carriers, the moment we fire we're dead..."

Reece slid out his bulging ray-gun clicking it into action. Abruptly the ship came to life. Hatches dropped open. Moments passed, seconds. A creature suddenly emerged followed by another. The enemy had finally manifested itself, captured in the periphery of their vision. Reece could now vaguely detect some kind of dialogue. It was muffled, indistinct, an alien tongue.

"That's them alright......"

"What are they?" Casper mumbled, his voice croaking with agitation.

"This isn't the best time for anthropological insight...but I would say man-made creatures, totally biological with vascular and pulmonary systems of some type...."

Reece paused studying them closely.

"Look at them, the extended larger frontal area of the skull indicates a highly intelligent systematic brain......highly developed cognitive faculties, greater conceptual capacity."

"And......?"

"And......we have to be extra careful, they have powerful neurological capabilities......an intelligent mind is capable of much trouble......"

A moment of weighted thought......

"So......what's the plan......?"

"Plan......?"

A faint smile flitted across Casper's masked features. He shook his head, gazing off into the distance. *"This isn't the best moment for jokes, Reece.....we need an organized strategy......"*

Slowly the two creatures re-entered the ship. Silence resumed; a penetrating silence. Reece blinked as a venomous wind blew around them. It soon died off.

"Let's move in, we'll take it as it comes......"

He gripped his ray-gun tightly.

"It won't be long before they are alerted to our presence......"

Rapidly crouching, half kneeling they moved over towards the ship, maintaining equilibrium across the uneven ground, ray-guns in hand balanced expertly. The ship now took on another form, transforming itself from a spherical shape to a squarer one, its alloys appearing to melt, twisting and expanding as if the frame of the ship had been subjected to sudden tremendous heat. After solidifying it began to glow faintly. An invisible energy field had been activated around it. They could almost trace it in the air, as if they had inner sensors capable of detecting changes in frequency. They paused a few meters away, and stood.

"Amazing......"

"Yeah," Casper replied in startled apprehension......eyes wide and curious.

"Look Casper, an open hatch...."

"Wait....," he muttered, halting Reece in his tracks..... *"Perhaps it's a trap......"*

"We'll chance it......"

As they entered, a long, ominous passageway snaked ahead of them. It was narrow and cold, dim floor lights leading the way down into the interior of the ship. Slowly they advanced, cautious and alert until they reached a door shutting off the passage abruptly. Reece pointed indicating the door. Halting they listened, acutely conscious of a light that shone through a thin aperture above and below. Casper slid to the floor, peering underneath....

"*Nothing......,*" he whispered looking up. "*Can't see anything at all......*" He returned to his feet, looking at Reece indecisively.

There was a long agonized pause. Reece remained silent, weighing up the situation. Then, with razor-like awareness he sensed, behind the door, the presence of life.

"*Casper......Get ready......*"

Instantly Reece slid the door open charging in. Standing before him were three creatures, faces convulsing in alarm. Rapidly he took aim, zeroing in on them......

"*Freeze......get back.*"

The creatures responded by moving into a huddle, clicking and squeaking......their multi-lensed eyes staring fiercely. Casper rushed over, waving his ray-gun with both hands....

"*Who sent you...?*" Reece demanded. "*Speak!*"

The creatures were terrified, uttering meaningless sounds.

"*It's futile, they can't......So what do you think.....R-Bomb carriers......?*"

"*Perhaps......I'll use the scanner......*"

Reece's hand flew to his belt activating the scanner. It buzzed; outcome negative.

"*It's registered clean......*"

"*Good, so what next......?*

There was no reply. Instead Reece began looking around the chamber, studying the baffling mass of machinery that surrounded him. Lights pulsed and flashed; hums and bleeps sounding at regular intervals. In the centre stood a narrow metal rod, a device, vertically orientated, almost to the same height as the humans themselves. Suddenly, one of the creatures reached for a long thin weapon. Instinctively Reece fired, targeting the cerebral region, blasting the creature to the floor, blue and white sparks of rippling light penetrating into it. He inched nearer, studying it at closer range, cradling his gun apprehensively......

"*Contact base......let them know we've tracked them......*"

Casper lowered his gun by degrees, snapping on the vidphone across his wrist. It hummed and sparked into life, flashing light against his mask. On the screen Duke's features were sharp and distinctive, even the scar on his lip that marred his face.

"*We've got them......one dead already.....two to go, there may be more.....so far operation running smoothly.....no complications......*"

"*Present location?*"

"*3.2 miles from launch.......on board an immobilized alien ship....These guys have a sinister plan going......*"

"*Any R-Bombs found?*"

"*Not yet Duke,*" he said, "*but I'm sure they have them onboard.....somewhere......*" His eyes roamed.

"*Okay, registered......current position stored. All clear......*"

Duke broke the connection. The image suddenly dimmed, vanishing moments later. There was silence for a time. Pulses raced. Reece was occupied in deep thought. The conduits of his brain calculating their next step......

"*Casper, I'll have to inspect the ship......there appears to be nothing here in what must be the control room......*"

"*Is it advisable....?*"

"*It's a must......*"

"*Don't stray too far,*" Casper cautioned. "*There could be a whole army of these things......*"

"*Don't worry......*"

Reece walked over towards the corner of the chamber where another door stood, outlined in a golden rust colour. Under the pressure of his fingertips, it slid open, disappearing into the wall. Ahead lay a passageway, dots of blue light marking the way down. Slowly he advanced, heavy boots echoing against the hard floor. He raised his gun above his shoulder and continued to move ahead with caution.

He grew breathless, hesitating. Visions of what could lie ahead flashed through his mind. Nervous sweat broke out across his face. Reaching the bottom he could progress no further; a door sealed off the passageway.

Bringing his ray-gun into position, he fired, its rays eating away at the hard metallic alloys, burning a neat hole through the door. The circular piece of smoking metal fell into the chamber ahead. Reece entered, waving his gun. No sound or movement. From the silvered ceiling, beams of light shone onto the floor continuously; a translucent light that radiated with brilliance. It seemed to him that its motion almost formed a pattern. Moving with care and trepidation, he passed through it as there was no way of avoiding it. Instantly his figure began to dim, wavering, fading until he was almost invisible; a glimmering shape of vague existence. At last he was through to the other side......

Suddenly he turned his attention to the long chamber in which he found himself. It was filled with electronic and mechanical components, nothing but gadgets, wires, and circuit boards spread out across a series of circular tables. To his left, he noticed a large container. He walked over and stood gazing into a swirling vat of bubbling liquid. It appeared they were planning to construct or develop something. Reece wondered, theorising. At once, he heard a sound. A vibration. Then silence. Although no one was in sight, he remained alert. He could almost sense the presence of others, an inner jolt; a subconscious intuition that warned him of danger.

Then, from a concealed sliding door two creatures appeared, armed with long thin weapons, as if they had materialized from out of nowhere. Before he knew it a red destruct beam flashed past him, missing narrowly, zapping against the wall of the chamber with a metallic clang. Then another zoomed past, inches from his head. Deftly, he twisted his body and rolled across the floor. Now kneeling, he took rapid aim and fired repeatedly. The rays hit their targets, penetrating deeply. Both creatures staggered for a while, until at last they fell onto the floor motionless. Reece's heart thumped heavily. He lowered his ray-gun and gradually regained equilibrium.

Standing up he refocused, and began scanning the chamber, rummaging through the pile of mechanical components, hunting cautiously, finding nothing, at least nothing of any immediate relevance. He paused wondering, then hurried back towards the control room. Running in he found it empty; Casper was gone along with the two creatures. Even the body of the one he had shot. Immediately, a great oppression came over him, a sense of doom. Hastily, Reece consulted his vidphone, but failed to connect....

"*Casper......*" he yelled, the rising pitch in his voice suppressed by the mask.

Waiting anxiously for a reply, doubts flooded his mind. There was nothing but silence, only the sound of working machinery. Rapidly he headed for the exit, towards the hatch, where the growing light of day revived him with hope.

"*Casper......Casper.....*"

The sound of his desperate echoes returned void. He turned gazing around at the desolate expanse, mountains, dust, and blinding sunlight. Again he attempted to work his vidphone but it was totally inoperative.

Moving back into the ship it suddenly roared into life, rumbling with power; the floor chugged under him. The hatch door began to close. He had seconds. He had to think and act fast. Caught in the grip of conflicting emotions he rushed for the exit, leaping out. With a hard thump, he fell colliding with the ground awkwardly. A cloud of arid dust engulfed him obscuring his vision. He waved it away, barely conscious. The roar outside was intense, its deafening noise causing him to regain awareness. Reece, now more alert, crawled away and lay at a safe distance, gazing over.....

The ground beneath began to shake.....jets roared as they burst into activity. The immense ship rose, gaining altitude, a great rushing sound filling the air. Soaring high into the atmosphere, Reece tracked its movement, eyes compellingly fixed upon it, but in a blink, it had disappeared, gone, heading out for deep space. Silence fell. A silence so abrupt it was startling. On the ground and in a daze, Reece attempted to contact base, but he began to drift into a state of unconscious......

It was night. Above, the moon lit the surface of Earth, cutting into the gloom. Stars stretched across the sky, infinite and tiny energetic dots of white. There was a bleep, followed by another. Reece's vidphone flashed into life...The sound roused him, breaking his solitude. His eyes opened, adjusting to the darkness.

"*Reece....this is Duke....do you copy....I repeat do you copy...?*"

The voice came to him as if from a great distance. Still dazed, he moved his hand wearily, gazing blankly at the brightly illuminated vidphone with blurred vision.

"*Yes......I copy,*" he murmured. His voice slurred....low and strained.

"Are you hurt?"

"No, I'm okay....but I was out cold for a time...."

He shook his head. The screen fuzzed then cleared.

"We've been trying to contact you for hours.....we almost gave up hope. Give me your precise location and we'll get a rescue team out there immediately.....Casper told us he searched for miles, but couldn't find you......"

"What....?" The pitch in his voice rose. His mind began to clear, slowly restoring his thoughts and faculties into a process of normality. *"You've heard from him..?"*

"He's with us, alive and well. He's at the medical centre undergoing the standard routine tests for after-surface exposure...."

Reece stood up, regaining strength, his dizziness fading. Sudden doubt assailed him.

"But....but I don't understand, that's not possible......he was taken up in the ship......at least that's how it seemed..."

"He got away......he re-entered two hours ago...."

Reece was puzzled, trying to make sense of it all. It just didn't seem to add up. He reflected back frowning, switching from scene to scene frantically, looking into one possibility after another. *'The ship, the creatures......the room full of wires, gadgets, circuit boards and mechanical components... What were they building? Perhaps a machine?'* he pondered further, deeper. *'A robot, an R-Bomb carrier perhaps...perhaps...?'*

"Duke, listen you've got to......"

Before he could complete his sentence the vidphone suddenly cut out......all sound, image and light with it. The blackness of night returned, and the ground beneath him shook violently. His mouth opened in a soundless scream, his eyes staring in blind horror......

Out in space, within the ship, a creature sat in the control room manipulating buttons and levers idly. It then dialled a series of numbers across the control module, raising the communication cone to its mouth......

"Commander, Mission accomplished......The R-Bomb robot carrier which replaced the human was perfect, constructed with high precision accuracy......identical to the human hostage....It's all set, R-bomb ready to explode at the trigger phase......"

"Great...how long before it detonates?"

The creature turned a dial, gazing at the screen......

"*It has Commander......it already has.....*"

Mind Blitz

THEY moved like ants, powerful and metallic. Robots were everywhere. Planet E, the new Earth was governed totally by machine along with all the other earth colonies within the solar-system and beyond. They had defeated humans; a long bitter war which had now come to an end. Special signals were emitted from the central governing base scanning the minds of man, all cephalic activity, electrical and chemical, thus giving robots complete control. All thoughts were continually extracted, analyzed then the complete gestalt; the ultimate robot mind invasion. The heterogeneous world had ended. The homogeneous had begun. Even dreams were recorded. The advertisement boards around the planet read, *'Pure thoughts only, Negative, could be punishable by death.'*

Detective Elio Decker, a Robot, had just flown in from Mars. Making his way out of the spaceport, he caught a Hover-Cab. It ascended into the atmosphere at a steady velocity, the City of New York slowly fading away. Achieving the correct altitude it glided horizontally, the driver allowing the autonomic circuit to make the journey. Exhausted, Elio pulled out his small metal container: R-stimulants. He took one, and within seconds was alert. He gazed mechanically into the evening twilight. In the distance he could see ships heading for outer space; tiny metallic glints lost in the red tinted sky.

Suddenly, the intercom across his steel wrist buzzed.

"We still haven't found him."

"Keep searching....I want him found soon."

The next day, a team of robot police beat down the door of an apartment on Wickers Street, New York.

"Jefferson Santa Cruz..." an officer yelled rushing in, his voice harsh and guttural. He clutched his long thin beam-rifle, pointing it, staring into a vacant room, other officers swarming behind........

"Damn, he's gotten away again."

The chief inspector walked over.

"Just wait till we get hold of him, he can't be too far....can you smell it?" he rasped with metallic revulsion, his mechanical eyes roaming, searching. The officer nodded with distaste. The human scent was still acutely present, bedcovers spread and creased. A can of shaving foam lay on the warm metal floor, a streak of foam seeping from it. Clothes were tossed

across the bathroom sink in a knot of confusion, a gold chain lying across it sparkling in the light. Feverishly, the team of police began inspecting, turning the room upside down holding their beam-rifles.

Down the street, concealed amongst a small crowd of noisy school kids, Jefferson darted towards the approaching red vehicle, sunlight dazzling his eyes, snow everywhere. The cold roused him, clouds of vapour puffing from his mouth.

"*Hurry, get in......quick,*" Athena cried, waving her heavily jewelled hand. The door opened automatically. He sat, slamming it behind him with force.

"*They just busted in......a whole team of those stinking machines....I caught a glimpse....they were everywhere....!*"

The air-car moved with power, ascending into the sky steadily.

"*Stay calm,*"....he said regaining his breath, his neck and white shirt damp with sweat. "*Do you have it on? They could track us otherwise........*"

She lifted her earlobe exposing the tiny black device. A signal breaker....

"*Are you absolutely sure it works?*"

"*Trust me as long as it's activated you're fine, it nullifies the signal.*"

She brushed back her brown locks grinning, almost gloating with achievement......

"*It's amazing to think that this small contraption allows my thoughts and ideas to remain mine, solely mine, and are not displayed in that damn control centre for robot consumption.....Can't believe how most of the population just accept it.......*"

He wiped his neck with a hanky, soaking perspiration, and replied......

"*They've been brainwashed Athena, slow progressive mind manipulation. It's the norm....the robots play on the notion of pure thinking.....to rebel means to have evil intentions, ideas.......evil thoughts....The general public have embraced it religiously......at least for now......In time, things may change.....*"

They landed in a field five miles outside the city centre, heavy tires marring the hard packed snow, dead trees frozen with winter chill.

"*How long before we reach the cottage Athena?*"

"*It's only a few miles from here.......*"

"*Good.*" He turned scanning the landscape; his mind deeply entrenched in thought.

At the cottage beside a blazing synthetic fire, Jefferson warmed his hands, his eyes bright in the firelight. The room itself contained nothing but a light grey sofa. Sections were torn and stained. The surrounding timber walls were dusty, cracked with age and neglect. The cottage location was ideal, locked away from the endless tide of noise and manic city life. No sound, no motion, nothing but snow covered nature engulfing them in all directions.

"How long have you had this place?"

"Years, goes down through generations……a bit of a relic…..."

He smiled. *"I see….."*

Her expression became serious, urgent.

"What are we to do……? They're going to get us sooner or later, especially with all their secret technology…they'll cover mile after mile of land until they reach us, we are hanging onto borrowed time………"

"Maybe……" His voice suddenly rose. *"If only we could get a ship out of here."*

"Where…?"

"Out of this solar system….…..there are a few remaining planets in our galaxy that still remain under the old law of free thinking…Ganymede is the only one in this solar system."

"Yes, but they are still all under Robot control..."

"We can't escape that Athena……they control everything."

He began pacing up and down the room in angered contemplation, bitter and dispirited. Tree branches slapped against the window, powered by the wind.

"I have correlated all the facts. Statistically most humans accept the mind blitz but there are growing numbers who want out….we need to reach these segregated groups and individuals before the special agents and police do………We need numbers if we are to up rise against the robots."

He paused. His cold grey eyes dilated.

"There are many that want to be human again……"

Athena shot him a confused look………..

"Human….?"

"Yes Athena….a part of being human is to have independent thought and for it to remain within the individual alone. At present we are nothing more than cattle, without free will, denuded, stripped from our ability to be…….."

He walked over to the sofa and sat, arms folded.

"Free will, the ability to act and think for one-self is what fundamentally separates us from all other living things, and makes us what we are, human....."

A sudden roar cut off his words in an instant. The cottage windows vibrated faintly, bits of hard accumulated ice breaking off and falling to the ground below. Jefferson darted to the window. He could see a patrol-air-car landing, green descent lights winking on and off, almost lost in the sparkling morning sunlight.

"Cops, quick, let's move...."

Her eyes widened.....her face turning chalk white with cold fear. Abruptly they turned and fled for an exit. Outside a team of four robots rushed towards the front door.

"Santa Cruz open up.........you have three seconds," one rasped sharply, his voice seeking to penetrate the thickness of the door. An interval of silence, then.....with a series of blasts from their beam-rifles, the door was consumed into nothingness. All that remained was a hovering cloud of greyish dust particles. From the sudden pressure, a window cracked, a fine web of hair line fractures splintering in all directions. They moved in with energy, mechanically, scanning and probing. The wood beneath them creaked and split, giving way to the immense metallic weight that besieged it.

At the back of the cottage, Jefferson and Athena darted out from an escape door, rushing furiously towards the forest, pushing branches out of the way in panic. As they moved deeper into the endless forest of silent towering trees, the wind battered against them, almost halting them in their tracks. Even the elements appeared to conspire against them. Finally they stopped, regaining breath in the chill winter air, staring, listening. Above, a flock of birds fluttered away breaking formation, their sound and motion unnerving.

"Jefferson......" Athena cried, her heart pounding, chest rising and falling with the effort of breathing. *"What do we do now?"*

Deftly, he snapped on his map-watch, fingers glued to the dials. Green lights lit, flashing dimly against his skin.

"Athena we can't go back.......If we keep moving north, we'll come to a road a mile away.....we're heading in the right direction for the city...."

"But it's too dangerous there......."

"What choice do we have?"

Suddenly, the four robot police appeared, fallen branches cracking, crunching and splintering beneath them, sunlight sparkling across the bare metal sections of their bodies.

"Arrest them…!" one yelled, his voice harsh and penetrating.

Two stormed over, one grabbing Athena, securing locks around her feet and hands. She was motionless, speechless, as if gripped by a paralysis. Her mouth gaped, lips trembling, eyes inflamed with muted urgency.

"You know your rights, don't you Sir?" the other said grabbing the signal breaker from Jefferson's earlobe and then driving a beam-rifle into his ribs. He jolted back, hands raised, the stark realization of defeat etched into his features. The robot's mechanical eyes were severe. Scanning Jefferson down, he took various readings.

"I think we should kill him……."

"No……we have strict orders to bring him back alive….."

The robot slammed his fist into Jefferson's face with decisive impact. He staggered back and forth until he fell heavily onto the hard snow. His head spun, his ears rang. Darkness and light engulfed him, fading and receding. The drifting sparks soon passed. He blinked regaining consciousness, gradual comprehension coming to him.

"Get up Santa Cruz, it's time….."

In the evening gloom, alive with sound and activity, the city of New York was glowing with light, glistening in the endless piles of white snow. Above patrol cars circled the sky, ghostly outlines of metal in motion disappearing into the cold night. Around the Police State headquarters, a strange murky haze hovered ominously. Jefferson sat inside, alone under bright penetrating cell lights in front of a bare metal table. He was rigid with apprehension. His head ached, each minute passing like a breathless hour. At the sound of approaching footsteps he swallowed weakly, hours of questioning had him in a daze. His heart began to palpitate. The door melted away. Detective Elio Decker walked in. He sat facing Jefferson.

"Santa Cruz we have blitzed Athena's mind, however we have been unable to probe your mind. Why……?"

Jefferson smirked.

"Answer me!" His voice rose as he regarded him, trying to fathom his reaction and ironically, his thoughts.

"What have you done with Athena?"

"She has been imprisoned awaiting trial.......Ever since the law came into effect five years ago you appear to have devised a way to cut off the signal.....remarkable....we have no file on you, nothing whatsoever. You do realise this crime is punishable by death.......?"

"Yes, but then again, to strip a human of his basic rights, to remove our individuality, our ability to think freely is death anyway, is it not......?"

"You are entitled to your opinion..."

"Am I?" Jefferson replied sarcastically. An interval of contemplation....

"The law is the law.......why would anyone rebel against it unless he or she is guilty of something evil?"

"Nonsense...! Each man is entitled to think and be as he chooses within the confines of his mind, and for him alone. To lock into people's thoughts is a form of control, it breaks the very essence of what we are...individuals..........humans."

"Santa Cruz, ever since we robots implemented the mind blitz, crimes have gone down from 85 percent to almost 3 in the New York state alone......People are forced to train their minds to think pure. When your thoughts and ideas are good, so too will be your actions........"

"Everyone has negative thoughts regardless.......it's a part of human nature...."

"Indeed....the system filters out the severe from the trivial. As a result we prevent crimes by, locking into people's minds. Prevention is better than cure...The benefits are enormous."

Jefferson opened his mouth, but didn't reply........

"We have a file on every human being, every thought, idea, belief, philosophy........"

The door melted away; a female robot officer walked in. She bent beside Elio and spoke, her focus fixed towards Jefferson as if ready to pounce.

"It's no use....we've kept trying and have still failed to lock in. We have only been able to gather basic encephalic data."

"Okay."

The female robot officer turned and left the cell....her heels clicking against the metallic floor. Elio shut his robotic eyes, pressing his hands together. He opened them suddenly.

"Here's the deal........."

Jefferson shuffled with interest, faint hope stirred him. Yanking out the signal breaker, Elio placed it on the table....

"Aside from this small contraption..." He pointed at it, keeping his eyes on him. *"What other method are you using to break the signal? If you disclose this information....."* He held back for a second as if jostling with an idea.... *"You'll be a free man. I'll even free Athena."*

Jefferson sat up, eyes wide with surprise and confusion...

"Obviously you understand you will have to leave the planet... there is no place for a person like you in this society....You're a fugitive....Your face has been all over the news.....however Athena will remain here."

An ice-cold feeling cut through him.

"Where will I go exactly....?"

"There are several planets outside our solar system, ones that remain with the old method of free thinking.....ones with soaring crimes rates and warped activity....However, if you are to remain within this solar system, your only option would be Ganymede......"

"What guarantees do I have, I can trust you......?"

Elio stood, his powerful metallic arms crossed.

"You have my word, but then again what other choice do you have?"

Jefferson bit away at his lip deep in thought.....

"Of course you would have to takeoff from Asia....it's the only continent that journeys to these particular planets, and Ganymede. An inter-continental cruiser will take you there....the Pacific tunnel is now open. It will drive you through the ocean into Asia from Vancouver. Well....are you going to talk.......?"

Jefferson ran his hand through his hair. He considered for a time, weighing up his words. Death or freedom depended on one little factor, it hung in the balance. He took a long deep breath, hesitating.

"There's an undetectable miniature device, a tiny device implanted within me which breaks the signal, and as a result synapse speed immediately increases, causing a rise in intelligence."

"Go on......"

"I built it in an underground base, alone. When swallowed it stores itself within the brain, in the Limbic system, exact location, Hippocampus. It can't be removed.....it works with immediate effect, there is no way of undoing it."

"The formula....?"

"I have it right here..."

"Where......?"

Jefferson pulled off his map-watch, pushing it across the metal table.

"Go into operations.......password DELTA/5."

He held it in his palm.

"Have you exchanged the formula with anyone else?"

"No..."

"How many of these devices have you made?"

"Just the one...but it was my intention to make many more..."

"I bet.....Tell me.....why were you wearing the signal breaker?"

"I wasn't certain how reliable the device was, I couldn't take any chances......but now I know it works perfectly.........."

"You're damn right about that...." he said emphatically.

He slammed the buzzer across the table. Instantly a male robot officer entered....

"Take this to CIP for analysis........"

"Yes Detective...."

Elio refocused, staring at Jefferson with conflicting emotions, admiration and cold resentment.

"You're a lucky man Santa Cruz...."

"Maybe so, but you do realise others will revolt in time....As we speak there are growing numbers who want out."

"Yes indeed and those very people are being tracked down and brought to justice. We robots control."

Jefferson snapped back.

"You can't win, you can't keep people in bondage forever......There will be a day when the citizens of this planet will fight for freedom, believe me, that day will come....society will eventually break down......"

"It's our job to prevent that, we have made sure such an up-rise will not occur. You have quite an imagination Santa Cruz......"

"Believe me, in time this mind invasion will come to an end. You can't control people forever......."

"Jefferson Santa Cruz, you are full of dreams....We robots have created a virtually crimeless society using mind control, right or wrong.......and like that, it shall remain....Just be glad you have had your life spared. All that awaits you now, is a distant sphere.....a place far away where you belong."

Inside the confines of a cold dark cell, Jefferson lay on a bed. Across his face the moonlight shone, as he gazed towards the barred window. Above, bitter stars slid in and out of the matted layer of fog. Hours had passed…..hours of contemplation, wondering what awaited him….what the future would bring. It would be hard living in another world. It would take time to adjust, time to mould in, but at least he would be free, free to be an individual. If only he had worked on reaching those segregated groups, the very ones that wanted out of the mind blitz, things could have been different on Earth…perhaps things would have changed. Perhaps he could have been the pioneer behind a huge revolt that would have seen the mind blitz end. All this was hypothetical…..the fact remained, it never happened……

On the horizon a streak of amber light appeared. The sun rose steadily, and in the growing light of day the city began to take shape and form. Rising higher and through broken cloud, the sun beamed down sparkling across lawns and sidewalks, a white blinding glare flooding the streets.

Outside the Police State headquarters, news reporters and angry crowds circled the building, suppressed by a team of robot-police forming a metallic shield. The city was alive, exploding into a torrent of sound and activity, swelling cries of indignation. Banners read: Kill the Criminal Santa Cruz…

In his cell, Jefferson stood at the sink, a robotic shaving arm cutting steadily into his stubble leaving his face fresh and clean. Two officers walked in accompanied by Elio.

"Are you all set….?"

He turned slowly.

"Yes I am…"

"You do realise there are hundreds of angry people outside…they all want you dead."

Jefferson nodded without expression, zipping up the blue uniform he had been provided with.

"Everything has been set up for you. You will get a rundown when you reach China, Shanghai…it's a long ride…you'll takeoff from there. Your new home will be Ganymede…we made the decision for you; a world of violence and free thinking, the

only place in this solar system like it. Come, it's time......... "He cut off sharply, reluctant to speak any further.

As the glass elevator reached ground level, it halted with a buzz. The sound of the angry crowds was now growing louder and more ferocious as they headed for the exit. Jefferson kept calm as he stepped out into the cold morning air, guided solely by the Elio. A wall of sound struck him, stinging his ears.

"Send Santa Cruz away......!" a toothless old man cried pointing, others following in chorus, chanting on and on, almost melodic.

"A good innocent man has no reason to hide his thoughts," a young woman blasted icily, bracing herself in the numbing cold, a dot of red glowing across both cheeks.

A group of youths pelted stones in his direction, a crew of reporters attempted to squeeze through the team of guarding police. Jefferson was gripped with fearless anger as he gazed around at the brainwashed crowds.

Reaching the cruiser the door slid open. He sat, his face pinched with fatigue, the driver setting the engines into motion. Elio stared at him for a time silently, his robotic eyes reflecting the sun like mirrors. He shut the door, the security bolts locking into place with a series of clicks. Inside all sound was cut off with immediate effect. Jefferson looked out, observing the hundreds of angry faces devoid of sympathy, some pointing, others curious and attentive.

'What hope was there for humanity,' he thought miserably, *'when your mind, thoughts and ideas are no longer your own?'*

Memoirs of Time

Boris Muller stood gazing at it with immense satisfaction. The time-sphere was designed with acute precision, a highly complex machine that would defy the laws of science and time.

"That's it, two years to the day and we have finally achieved our objective....this device represents a thousand years of science.....and mathematics....."

He turned with suave authority and walked over towards Claude, hands behind his back, analysing, thinking.....his hair wild and grey, bits of stubble poking from his chin.

"Can you imagine....this machine is capable of carrying a human not only into the past, but also into the future...but it's the past that interests me at present......"

He smiled....confidence emanating from his eyes....his geniality and wonderfully convoluted mind clearly displayed on his countenance.

"To have found the key that unlocks the door of time is possibly the greatest achievement of man. The past, present and future is frozen in time and space.....with this machine we can unlock that door....enter in and see into the future.....move into the past......"

"Yes Boris, but I'm still concerned. We need to look at the possible consequences, the possible dangers. It's high risk. Your presence alone could alter history......the present, and in turn, the future. You could start a never ending time shift. A chain reaction...."

"Don't allow your thalamic impulses to take control. Existence is a risk. Remember, risk is the key factor in success...You need to change your mind-set. To make history demands risk. I'm only going to briefly observe, nothing more. Observing is a minor risk. I will visit ancient China, ancient Egypt, Constantinople....the Byzantine period, and medieval England...."

Boris paused.....then continued...

"The food, drink and medicine that we consume each day are plagued with risk and severe collateral effects. Preservatives, sweeteners and chemicals that are altering the body at a genetic level; causing cancers, destabilising the balance of neurotransmitters, serotonin, dopamine....giving rise to neurological problems...depressions, psychosomatic disorders..... If we are to make history, we need to be devoid of fear...."

He was caught in thought...looking around his workshop, bolts and screws lying all around...

"Time travel.....illegal, forbidden... Those were the words from authorities when they had heard about our work, our project. Man has always been frightened to venture

into the unknown...."

A few moments of silence passed......

"*Claude......?*" He looked into his eyes, cold and hard...devoid of fear...

"*It's time to put to a test this mind-blowing theorem of space-time continuum......*"

A period of time elapsed......

All at once the time-sphere materialized. Claude drew breath, pushed back his hair and walked over to it in awe. Lights flashed and flickered, lighting Boris's face as he sat in front of the bank of controls deactivating the machine.

"*You're back.......it worked....!*"

Boris pressed the eject button, releasing the door, with it the scent of the past. He stepped out from the cold metallic sphere. Claude's eyes lit with anticipation.

"*Well.....what happened....?*"

"*I was there, back in time as incredulous as it seems. The minute I pressed the button everything went black in an incomprehensible flash, as if time had ceased for a moment...then suddenly light...a blinding light...and in the forming light, the landscape before me began to take shape and form....*"

Boris's face was alive, alive with radiance. His expression said it all with muted clarity.

"*I saw Ancient China, during the Shang dynasty, 1677 BC, the buildings, the landscape, and their wonderful costumes. I saw Ancient Egypt during the early period of Cleopatra's reign, 51 BC, the pyramids, the Nile....people going about their daily activities....I saw the glorious city of Constantinople, the Byzantine Empire or otherwise known as the Eastern Roman Empire, 395 AD. My last stop was Medieval England, 550 AD.....the Anglo-Saxons. I stood and simply observed what I could without being noticed......It's amazing to think how time has changed things...how technology and knowledge has revolutionized the world...yet there is a common element that unifies man throughout history and time.....*"

"*Which is....?*"

"*Man is still in search...*"

"*Of....?*"

"*Meaning...the meaning of our existence...Since the dawn of man, we have searched for meaning!!! The essence of our being...the notion of existence...The Cynics of ancient*

Greece grabbled with the idea....great philosophers throughout the ages thought long and hard...Socrates, Antisthenes, Plato, Aristotle....but it seems we are none the closer to unravelling the puzzle....the puzzle of life...."

"*Purpose, the meaning of life and what lies beyond, are subjective Boris...*"

"*Yes...but that's only personal opinion.....there can be only one absolute definitive truth as to why....*"

Claude rubbed his jaw in thought......

"*Why these sudden existential thoughts......? What prompted this sudden metamorphosis......?*"

"*I guess I've always been interested in philosophy, metaphysics, metaphysical cosmology, ontology...the universe, how it got here. It's incredible to think of all the billions of people that lived, and died.....the cycle of life....an ongoing conveyer belt. What absurd purpose could man have in this infinite universe? What role does he play? What propelled life into being? We grow old and die due to the movement of time. Man struggles to remain young. Why? Aside from the obvious, it's due to the fact that deep down within the subconscious of man we associate ageing with death. Hence to remain young gives man a temporal feeling of immortality....and yet inevitably death awaits us all. Is it death that gives life its meaning? Perhaps we live on, if so, we are immortal, eternal.*"

Claude stood in silence, assimilating Boris's words......

"*These are not rhetorical questions Claude. They need to be answered if we are to encapsulate the meaning of our existence.... I never forgot the final words of my grandfather....he had such a profound unifying concept of life.*"

Boris paused, eyes distant and reflective.

"*Man is held within the sphere of time and space...but beyond it lies another realm......*"

He Dreams Planet Earth

The giant rotating sphere that was Earth shone brilliantly. Luna's two week period of darkness was bleak, earthlight somewhat illuminating its barren surface. The two week diurnal cycle would soon follow, the Sun beating down mercilessly. Daylight was much brighter and harsher than the Earth's. No atmosphere to scatter the light, and no ozone layer to repel the sun burning ultraviolet light.

Inside his oxygen pumped lunar home Brent Juskowiak sat contemplating, thinking about Imperial Earth. For years he'd longed to be there and see its majestic forests and landscapes. The images burned in his mind. He pictured the Himalayas, the Atlantic Ocean, the pyramids of Egypt, the Great Wall of China. They all soon faded into an unreachable haze. Sadly, he rose from the bed and walked over to the window gazing into the lunar darkness towards Earth. Within seconds his father walked into the bedroom.

"Brent, I've just finished my book..... Three hundred pages explaining the fundamental nature of being and the world... A book like this is desperately needed on Earth...."

Brent was unresponsive, his eyes fixed into the void...

"What's wrong son.....?"

"Dad, I would love to see Imperial Earth...even to spend a day there....after all we are its descendants."

"Son, we have had this discussion before...."

His dad walked over, head down. Resting his hand on his son's back he looked out into the darkness. In the distance, he could vaguely see one of the lunar city structures.

"Son, I understand how you feel, but the Moon broke away from Earth's hold for a valid reason. Since the moon's independence there has been peace. Our government is centred on theism, Christian theism; Earth's is atheistic, pagan in nature. They may control all the planets within our solar-system and beyond, but we stand alone as a jewel in space, the only theistic sphere in the galaxy. The supreme power that governs Earth and all its colonies takes its route from many different civilisations and groups throughout time, starting with the Babylonian and Egyptian mystery cults, Kabbalistic mystery religions, the Gnostics, the Assassin cult or Ḥashshāshīn, the Knights Templar...Jacques de

Molay, the Jesuits...St. Ignatius of Loyola and so on. The power that controls has stripped mankind of free will. They control society through mind control. They emit special signals that scan the minds of man, highly complex signals, which have the capacity to extract all cephalic data. These signals are able to translate brainwave patterns into words. It's occultic in nature. Their excuse, mind control prevents crime; it's the ultimate crime prevention. The citizens of Earth have embraced it religiously. The French Philosopher Rene Descartes once said... 'Except our own thoughts, there is nothing absolutely in our power.' Son, if you remove freedom of thought man becomes a machine, a robot. Remember even God gave man free will."

His father paused. He rubbed his long white beard, his old eyes calm and reflective.

"I think the only remaining affinity between us and them is that the Moon is in synchronous rotation with Earth, tidal locking, and that the Moon's gravitational influence produces the ocean tides. Forget Earth son."

His dad patted him on the back then walked out. Brent reflected.....Maybe one day things will change he thought, but for now Imperial Earth remained nothing but an unapproachable planet....

The Edge of Eternity

He was lost in the vastness of space amongst the infinite stars. In the silence Alexis Falco lay back and closed his eyes. He'd completed his six months work assignment on the red planet, building the Mars-based radars which were used to discover asteroids. Powerful computers would calculate their orbits: all data and information was then stored. From the strength of the radar-echo, asteroid diameters were attained. Many asteroids were lost to the Sun, its gravitational field capturing the giant high velocity rocks.

Alone on the small ship with only the two pilots aboard, Alexis contemplated his journey as he briefly opened his eyes and read the data screen. Earth and Mars were currently at their closest points, separated by a distance of 55 million kilometres. The journey will be quicker at this distance, he thought. His departure had come at the perfect time. Mars had finally gained its independence from Earth. Much tension had grown between the two planets. All humans born on Mars were no longer classified human, but were known as Martians despite the biological and neurological essentials that made man. Through the side window Alexis gazed into the darkness. His eyes grew heavy. Rapidly he fell into a deep sleep as the ship moved fluidly through the silence of deep space.

Days passed.... The ship approached Earth with a roar. It plunged rapidly into its atmosphere manoeuvring for descent. Planet Earth glowed with splendour. The sun sparkled with brilliance, the ever present nuclear reactor. Alexis sat up. He was almost home. Green fields slowly came into focus, the flow of life on terra. Now, only meters away, the ship lost power. Betrayed by gravity it fell and hit the ground at a tremendous force sliding violently across the runaway, blazing out of control. Fire raged as it came to a halt. Then silence..........

Through the thick darkness of the unconscious world Alexis opened his eyes. Instantly he sensed the presence of another person.
"Mr Falco you were very close to death...."
Alexis looked up. Standing before him was an old man, casually dressed with piercing blue eyes.

"Your ship crashed killing both the pilots. Miraculously all you have is a few bruises and cuts but you will need to remain in hospital for a while."

Alexis lay upright looking around the private room. He began to recollect his journey from Mars, the accident and his final minutes of consciousness....

"I guess it wasn't my time. Who are you anyway? Are you a doctor?"

"No, I'm a Pastor."

Alexis was startled, his eyes narrowing with curiosity.

"Why are you here?"

"I often visit sick patients. You're not the first."

The pastor inched closer to the bed.

"Mr Falco what do you think would have happened to you had you died?"

There were a few moments of silence. A ray of sunlight filtered into the room.

"What do you mean?"

"Have you ever wondered what lies beyond?

"At death we cease to exist."

"That's the world's view, the atheistic doctrine that sadly governs our world today. But unfortunately this theory fails at so many levels; in fact it's in diametric opposition with science. Energy cannot be destroyed."

Alexis rubbed his eyes. "I'm an educated man, a top engineer. I'm aware of that."

"Ask yourself this, at death, what happens to that invisible energy of the brain known as consciousness? The first law of thermodynamics, the conservation of energy states; energy cannot be created or destroyed but can be transformed from one form to another. The implications are vast....We are immortal. Physics teaches this irrevocably."

Alexis lay in absorbed attention.

"The question now is what lies beyond death? There is another dimension beyond this three dimensional space we inhabit. There is a spiritual realm that is very real. In fact this realm can be deemed as the ultimate reality."

"Pastor, how can you speak with such certainty...the bible and all other religious books have no relevance with today's world. Science and reason has reformed man. The French revolution back in 1789 was the turning point in human history.....The Enlightenment, the Age of Reason, the cultural movement of intellectuals. There were many great Masonic leaders of the Enlightenment...Voltaire, Pope, Mozart, Frederick the Great, Benjamin Franklin, George Washington. There were so many great minds involved with its development: Francis Bacon, Gottfried Leibniz, Sir Isaac Newton, Baruch Spinoza, Joseph-Louis Lagrange."

"Mr Falco, science needs God. You simply can't remove God from the equation. The French revolution was an attempt to destroy theism, but it failed. The statue of Liberty takes its route from this attempt; it represents the light of reason and science."

"But how can you believe in the bible? Can you honestly believe in Adam? Can you truly believe he was made to live eternally on Earth?"

"Actually the bible doesn't teach this. Many young earth creationists believe that Adam was created as an immortal being, that is he was intrinsically designed to live forever, and that his sin, disobedience to God's commandments, resulted in the initiation of his death and the death of every other living thing. But what do science and the bible actually say about this? The laws of the universe are in diametric opposition to this notion. Not to mention that from a biblical perspective: if Adam were created immortal before he sinned, what was the purpose of the tree of life found in the Garden of Eden? It's important to understand that Adam could have lived forever by feeding on God's constant support of life. This is what the tree of life represented. Now, the law of decay, the second law of thermodynamics says that all life in this universe will cease, this includes the death of the entire universe itself. This is due to increasing disorder and dissipation of heat. This fundamental law affects virtually everything that happens in our universe. Now regarding the bible's view, it clearly states that order came into the world, the law of decay, well before the fall of mankind. Just read the creation story in Genesis."

Silence fell.........

"Mr Falco, immortality is not possible in this universe since the universe itself will eventually die without God's intervention. The second law of thermodynamics guarantees that physical beings cannot live eternally. Now regarding the bible... Genesis 1 tells us how God created the universe and life on earth in a simplified form. The last of creation was Man, created in His image. Although God had created previous hominid species on earth, modern humans were the first to possess a spirit. This is key....It gave modern man, Adam and Eve, the capacity to communicate with God. Man could now have a relationship with the Creator. However it is important to note that God had to give man a choice. True love always requires this. God wanted Adam and Eve to love and trust Him by choice. The only way to give this choice would have been to command something that was not allowed: don't eat from the tree of knowledge, good and evil. Knowledge means experience. God's ultimate plan was to have relationship with mankind without the influence of evil. Mankind today still has the same choice as Adam and Eve. We can gain the knowledge of evil by directly participating in it. This is known as sin. The other choice is to love God with all our heart and avoid evil."

Alexis looked at the Pastor.... both admiration and conflict emanating from his eyes.

"You're a very deep man..... Tell me, how would you as a believer counteract the eternity of matter theory...that is, the universe has always existed. All the citizens of Mars hold this view rigidly?"

"As mentioned..... the second law of thermodynamics holds that over time, under normal circumstances, all systems left on their own tend to become disordered, and corrupted. In other words all things are subject to decay, deterioration, living or not, biological or mechanical, and finally, are destroyed. This process cannot be avoided; death itself is a manifestation of this law. It is the immutable metaphysical law of the universe."

The pastor paused momentarily....

"Mr Falco, the entire universe is unavoidably proceeding towards cosmic death. This life-death cycle clearly reveals that there had to be a beginning to everything in the universe including the universe itself. In light of this, the eternity of matter theory makes no sense. God is the genesis of life, the creator. He dwells in eternity, outside the sphere of time and space."

"So what's your view on evolution?" Alexis asked.

"Sadly, it ignores this fundamental law of physics. It totally contradicts it.

Evolution the highly complex process says that disordered, dispersed, and lifeless atoms and molecules spontaneously came together over time, in a particular order resulting in the formation of very complex molecules......proteins, DNA, etc....In other words, life as a whole simply evolved by itself under natural conditions. The second law of thermodynamics contradicts this mechanism. No highly complex organic molecule can ever form spontaneously, but will rather disintegrate."

"I see your point......"

"To summarize....naturalistic/atheistic Evolutionism...evolution that removes God from the equation requires that physical laws and atoms organize themselves into increasingly complex and beneficial ordered arrangements over time. The second law of thermodynamics says this is not possible. Highly complex, ordered arrangements tend to become disorderly over time and less complex. In other words, there's a downhill spiral at work regarding life throughout the universe. However, there are some people today who believe God is the mechanism behind evolution...theistic evolutionists. But this is another subject matter altogether...."

Alexis was gripped in deep thought. The expression on his face and the glow in his eyes said it all.

"Mr Falco it's time for me to go....but I'll leave you with these final words. We all live on the edge of eternity. Life can cease at any moment. You were designed with a purpose...that purpose is to know God....in fact everything in the universe is designed with a purpose. Teleonomy, information stored within the genes of a living thing is one of the greatest proofs of God's existence. Remember Matter, itself, is not creative........."

A few weeks had passed. Alexis stood on the balcony of his apartment on the fiftieth floor. He gazed into the night sky, cigarette in mouth. Hard rain fell. Lightning and thunder lit the sky. The profound discussion he'd had with the Pastor had left him questioning life, the universe and its meaning. It was time to make a definitive choice. This choice would require a serious life change. Even the humans born on Mars would need to hear this message, even though terra no longer recognized them as human. Human meant to have a spirit, a soul regardless of where you are born, he thought. He pondered for a while, and decided it was time. Inching to the balcony he dropped his cigarette and watched it fall towards the city below.............

Lightning Source UK Ltd
Milton Keynes UK
UKOW05f1549240714

235704UK00001B/10/P